BAD
FICTION

Also by Rebecca Ley

Sweet Fruit, Sour Land

BAD FICTION

REBECCA SARAH LEY

THE BOROUGH PRESS

The Borough Press
An imprint of HarperCollins*Publishers* Ltd
1 London Bridge Street
London SE1 9GF

www.harpercollins.co.uk

HarperCollins*Publishers*
Macken House, 39/40 Mayor Street Upper
Dublin 1, D01 C9W8, Ireland

First published by HarperCollins*Publishers* 2026

1

Copyright © Rebecca Sarah Ley 2026

Rebecca Sarah Ley asserts the moral right to be identified as the author of this work

A catalogue record for this book is available from the British Library

Hardback ISBN: 978-0-00-871305-8
Trade Paperback ISBN: 978-0-00-871306-5

This novel is entirely a work of fiction. The names, characters and incidents portrayed in it are the work of the author's imagination. Any resemblance to actual persons, living or dead, events or localities is entirely coincidental.

Set in Adobe Garamond Pro by HarperCollins*Publishers* India

Printed and bound in the UK using 100% Renewable Electricity by CPI Group (UK) Ltd

All rights reserved. No part of this publication may be reproduced, stored in a retrieval system, or transmitted, in any form or by any means, electronic, mechanical, photocopying, recording or otherwise, without the prior written permission of the publishers.

Without limiting the exclusive rights of any author, contributor or the publisher of this publication, any unauthorised use of this publication to train generative artificial intelligence (AI) technologies is expressly prohibited. HarperCollins also exercise their rights under Article 4(3) of the Digital Single Market Directive 2019/790 and expressly reserve this publication from the text and data mining exception.

For Theo

The first phase

Posted by aw0mbofonesown

AITA for telling my male friends their stories of sexual harassment don't count?

I was at the pub last weekend with a group of friends and by the end of the night, I was the only woman left. I don't know how the topic came up, but suddenly the group started sharing their stories of when they've been preyed upon by women (in a sort of, 'it happens to us too' way).

I sat there feeling intensely awkward as they discussed female colleagues who'd touched their arms or joked about giving them a pay rise if they went on a date with them. One of my friends told a story about his female tutor at university. Allegedly, she invited him round to her house and offered him several glasses of wine until he'd nodded off. When he woke up, she was touching him. He said he didn't like her romantically, so she'd spent the rest of the term making his life a misery (incessant calls, emails, and then when he didn't respond, had marked his assignments down).

Firstly, I'm not sure this even happened or if he was just jumping on the bandwagon of the conversation. Secondly, if it did, am I the asshole for saying it's just not the same as if it was the other way around? Also, shouldn't they save these woe-is-me conversations for each other and not talk about it in front of women who've inevitably had much worse experiences?

1.5k comments

One

Alice

We gathered in the bookshop like churchgoers at the Sunday service. It was a warm but imposing place to host our first literary event as a tutorial group, celebrating a former student from our course. Most of us went for the lukewarm wine laid out in rented glasses.

I looked at the stack of signed books piled up on a table and fingered one of the spines. 'It's amazing, isn't it?' I said.

Walt was drinking orange juice next to me.

'The whole thing gives me anxiety,' he said. 'Every time I walk into a bookshop it's like a reminder of how many books I'll never read before I die.'

Stella blinked at him.

'Every time I read a book, I feel better about everything.' She was older than us and had a kind-hearted Scouse twang. She took a sip of her red wine and pulled the end of an unseasonable pale blue scarf she'd wound around her neck. 'Even if the book isn't very good. I sleep better, I eat better, I find myself inhabiting a world that I don't want to end and if the book is really good, it follows me round all day. I can't help telling everyone that they should read it, even if I don't think they'd particularly like it. It becomes as much a part of my life as anything that's ever happened to me. It's not that

I find bookshops endlessly inspiring, but they don't make me want to *die*.'

Walt pointed out that he hadn't said he wanted to die, only that sometimes reading felt futile, especially when he forgot entire books he'd actually read.

'When I was younger, I used to devour them, staying up late into the night to get to the end. It was mainly to get my mind away from my mother, but also it was just a lot of fun. Now I end up picking books I feel I should read and hardly enjoy any of them.'

'If the world of literature is so uninspiring,' I asked him, 'why do you want to write?'

He shrugged, downing his orange juice. The pulp stuck to the sides of the plastic cup, and he dipped a finger in to clear the edge, then sucked it.

'I think I'm pretty good at it.'

'No one becomes a writer because they think they're just good at it,' Stella said. 'People become writers because they think they're better at it than everyone else.'

She had on patterned tights and a red mini skirt, exactly the kind of thing I'd grown up thinking a writer should wear, which now felt strangely infantile. Then I reminded myself, the only thing that mattered is what a writer wrote.

Stella went to bag herself a seat before the talk began, and Walt admitted that he did sometimes think he was better than everyone else. 'But so does everyone, I'm just saying it out loud.'

I would usually find this kind of admission loathsome, but it disarmed me. I'd only known him for a couple of weeks, but I already felt that he was a straightforward person, who said what he felt and meant it. He also had a handsome, open face, that got better the longer I spent with him. In short, we were becoming friends.

Then he said: 'Like, what was that whole "yes, and" thing earlier? I didn't realise we'd be doing improv.'

In one of our first classes of the term that day, our writing tutor,

Robert, had asked us to workshop a plot together. The only rule was that you had to reply to everyone's idea with 'yes, and'. Robert wrote radio plays and taught us while he was trying to finish his third novel. He had mentioned his background in theatre, where as a playwright and actor 'you are nothing but a piece of shit to anyone'.

Robert smelt of shampoo and stale coffee. The more animated he had become about inciting incidents, the stronger the smell of his warm, sour breath in the air. I had waited for the game to end while Walt stayed silent next to me, his mouth open in unashamed incredulity.

'Oh Alice, I kept looking at your face.' Walt gave me a smile that at first I had been stunned by, but then quickly got used to, like eating five cream buns in one go. 'It was so wound-up and disbelieving it made the whole class sort of bearable.'

'I'm glad I could be a source of amusement for you.'

He nudged my arm. 'Tell me you didn't hate every second of it. Tell me.'

'Apparently I don't need to.'

'You have a very readable face. Like a dog or a child. You're doing it now,' he said, putting a finger in front of my nose. 'Did you know you have a line between your eyebrows that really settles in when you're walking around campus, lost in your thoughts?'

His own face was easy to read too, with all the open amusement of someone who makes themselves laugh. I didn't tell him this. Instead, I said: 'I wouldn't have taken you for a stalker.'

He ignored me, and went on, 'But now the line is gone, and it's like looking at a different person. The colour of your eyes makes your whole face seem friendlier when you want it to, like an evolutionary tactic for people to give you food and attention. But when you don't, they go almost black, and tell everyone to fuck off.'

'What colour are they now?' I took another sip of my wine, very aware of my own face. I felt an itch below my left eyebrow and reached up to scratch it.

He smiled. 'Don't go getting a big head, I didn't say that your eyes were beautiful or anything.'

'Just complex and thought-provoking and something you've been mulling over.'

'Like crop circles.'

I laughed and he told me I was getting red wine teeth.

'The analogy about crop circles makes sense,' he said, 'because there could definitely be a whole conspiracy theory dedicated to your eyes. They're oddly compelling.'

'It's hacky to talk about a woman's eyes,' I told him, but he shook his head.

'Not when you're not coming on to them. I'm analysing them objectively, like a doctor looking for a smudge on a bit of film.'

The head of our course appeared at the front of the room, carrying a glass of wine and a book, ready to take her seat as chair for the evening. Her hair was in artful disarray, an elegant clip holding it in place. It would've looked old-fashioned on anyone else, but she wore being in her fifties lightly. It made me feel excited to grow up and start my real life: the one with semi-precious jewellery, Radio 4 and the confidence that comes from getting away with something.

I wanted to go and say hello to her before the talk began, but when I suggested it, Walt sniffed derisively.

'As if Sofie Muller gives a shit about us in the real world.'

I decided it would show enthusiasm to introduce myself properly before our first class with her that week, so I walked up to her and told her my name was Alice. 'I was the one in the interview who said *The Bell Jar* was my favourite book, and afterwards I thought that sounded so trite,' I said.

She touched a manicured finger to one of her lobes to check her jade earring was still in place and said, 'I remember you. You wore a dress that matched the furniture.' Her nails were like candied almonds.

I felt my face grow hot, remembering the shade of lilac identical to the fabric chairs in the seminar room. It was strange to be up close to her again. I tried to calculate how many writers I'd be able to identify walking down the street. She'd done just enough TV appearances and book festivals that most people would give her a second glance.

'I love your work,' I added, for something to say.

She nodded.

'Yes.'

I waited for her to accommodate the awkwardness of the conversation, but no follow-up came. I attempted to mirror her expression of bored indifference. I wanted to try again. I opened my mouth to tell her which of her novels had truly devastated me (would I muster up the courage to tell her that *A Bird Came Down* had made me sit on my bathroom floor and cry?), but she'd already transferred her attention to a man approaching her.

He looked only a few years older than me, but I was surprised at the idea he was one of her readers, who were mostly women. I turned to a nearby bookcase, pretending to be interested in Cosy Crime.

'Sofie,' the man said. Instead of fawning over her, he just stood there. I glanced back and saw she was smiling at him in polite expectation.

'Hi there,' she said, matter-of-factly.

'It's me,' he pointed to his chest as though he could've meant someone else.

Sofie looked around in the hopes of an explanation. 'Sorry, I don't think . . .'

He said his name, incredulous, and told her that she'd taught him for an entire year. He had written a story about Alcoholics Anonymous that she'd said was truly life changing.

'How interesting. Do you still drink?' she asked.

He shook his head, letting out a deep throaty sound that made me worry he was about to be sick. 'You know I never . . . Sofie.' He put a hand up to his face. I waited for him to feel embarrassed, to back away in excruciated silence. He didn't move.

'You mustn't take it as an insult. I have so many students. Did you carry on writing?'

'No.'

I moved a few steps away and took out my phone to pretend I was checking on some important correspondence.

'What a shame. Are you here for the book launch?' Sofie said. 'It's by one of our most talented alumni.' Her voice was soft, but with a calm, steady authority.

I risked another glance and saw him shake his head.

'I saw that you would be here. I thought it was about time I showed my face at one of these things.'

She was nodding, trying to move away.

'What's the book about?' he asked.

'Sex,' she said crisply, looking around for someone else to talk to. It was clearly an attempt to shut the conversation down, but it seemed to have the opposite effect.

'That's a bit glib.'

'You wouldn't think so if you'd read it.' She took a sip from her wine glass. 'Will you excuse me, it's almost time to begin.' She turned to a woman putting a water bottle next to her seat. 'Why is everyone so obsessed with hydration these days? Those little plastic bottles the students insist on suckling during class, it's like they can't let go of their mother's nipples.'

She laughed and went to walk away, but the man put a hand on her arm and I saw her flinch, the first time she had lost her composure.

'I've been thinking about you a lot recently,' he said. She looked at his hand, offering no indication that she'd heard what he'd said. 'Or rather, about *The Arrival*. The book you wrote the year you taught me.'

'And what year was that?'

He removed his hand from her arm now that he had her attention. He told her the year in a deliberately exaggerated voice. 'When

I read it, I couldn't stop thinking about it for months afterwards. I thought about contacting you, but . . .'

She moved a loose strand of hair away from her face.

'That's remarkable,' she said. 'I wrote it so long ago, it's almost like a dream.'

The man was undeterred. 'You really don't remember me?'

She frowned at him, saying nothing, and I wondered if he was going to point out what he thought made him so memorable. As I stepped back to let people take their seats at the front, I studied him: he was handsome, perhaps notably so, but his face was hard with anger. What did he care about his old writing tutor when he had that strong brow, that pouty mouth?

'I hope you found the course useful, anyway,' Sofie said eventually.

'You must remember that year,' he said. 'You just have to. The night you had us round for wontons and *Working Girl*? You know that night.' A woman laughed beside me and I missed Sofie's murmured response. 'There were only ten of us that year,' he carried on, shaking his head in disbelief. 'It wasn't like a dream at all.'

Sofie looked confused, hesitating, like she was weighing up her options. Then she smiled, tapped the side of her glass, and loudly encouraged everyone to take their seats. The man went to touch her arm again and she moved away, sitting at the front of the room and putting her wine glass by her feet.

He brushed past me as I moved towards the back of the room. I took my seat between Walt and Stella and watched him slip out, the door's bell jangling as he disappeared. He seemed hurt to be forgotten, to have not made an impression. It made me want to be someone she remembered.

I had delusions. But so does everyone.

We listened to a lengthy introduction about the writer's time on the course and her newly published debut. Walt's leg started jiggling beside me, but I couldn't tell whether it was from boredom or irritation. Sofie questioned the author about her writing practices for a while, then during a reading that had already lasted five minutes Walt tapped me on the knee and whispered that he was going for a walk. I tilted my head towards the front of the room. 'It's not done yet,' I whispered back.

I need air, he mouthed at me, and slipped from his seat. I felt my body rise involuntarily to follow him, and I marched past the books to the front of the shop. Outside, Walt was standing on the street looking at his phone. He glanced up as I approached him. 'You came,' he said, as though it was a relief.

'I have no idea why.'

He swiped away from a stream of messages and clicked the lock button. 'You were thinking that the one thing better than reading books and talking about books and spending a whole evening listening to Sofie Muller talk about books is . . .' he thought about this. 'Pancakes.'

'Pancakes?' It was endearing how he said the word, like it was the name of a family pet.

'I know a place around here that makes giant filled crêpes with the weirdest ingredients. Honey and pepperoni and every kind of cheese and baked apple and caramelised banana.'

'There's nothing weird about banana.'

'Let's go then.'

I paused.

'I promise that the pancakes will sustain you more than any novel ever has.' He raised his hands in admission. 'Don't get me wrong, I get it. Writing is like sex. When you're in the moment, it feels amazing and then afterwards you wonder what was possessing you at the time. Only, when you write, the doing it only makes the desire worse.' He pointed down the street in the direction of the restaurant. 'When you're hungry, you can just eat pancakes and feel better.'

'*Yes, and* sick afterwards,' I said.

He grinned, taking the crook of my elbow and leading me away from the bookshop. '*Yes, and* happy, sick and happy.'

I smiled back, my boots tottering on the dark cobblestones. '*Yes, and* I'll wipe the tears of happiness from your face.'

He let out a small cackle. '*Yes, and* . . . oh God, it's such a load of bollocks, isn't it? If Robert hadn't written a novel, I'd absolutely pity him.'

It was dark outside and the yellow glow from the streetlights illuminated the steam from kitchen pipes in the houses around us. I felt glad to be going out to eat with someone who made me laugh just as the season was changing. Despite what he'd said that evening, Walt felt the same as the rest of us. The thought struck me as singular and sad: without writing, everything we did and said would be pitiable.

The restaurant was small, but we managed to find a table tucked into a corner. A candle dripped wax down an empty green wine bottle and I started to pick at its cool edges as soon as we sat down.

Walt ordered us two Dutch beers without asking me what I wanted. I opened my mouth to complain but he said I should trust him. I felt oddly formal to be sitting opposite him, especially when he started quizzing me about what my parents did and whether I had any siblings. I explained that I had a sister who was a minor character in my life because she'd moved away to get married. The older I got, the more I would think about how she tortured me when we were little, and the more it bothered me that she clearly never thought about it.

'Tortured you how?' he said.

'She made my life a living hell, actually, pointing out everything that was wrong with me all the time, getting me in trouble with my parents and accidentally on purpose locking me in my room for hours on end.' Just the usual sibling stuff.

'Sure, but normally people grow out of it and form an adult relationship, right?'

'She was so much older than me that by the time that could have happened, she'd already decided to move to the other side of the world. Now we see each other once a year and hardly ever speak.'

'Have you ever spoken to your parents about it?'

I only shook my head. They weren't people who talked about things beyond what they'd done that day or whether the rain would hold out until teatime.

'I'm sorry,' he said. 'I don't have siblings, so I always imagined they'd be an endless source of joy. But maybe having parents who are emotionally closed off isn't such a bad thing? My mother offers up every moment of social intercourse from her life, every bowel movement. I know who she lost her virginity to and what age her periods stopped.'

I took a sip of the dark beer the waiter had put in front of us. 'I'd love a mother like that. I'd love parents with personality, rather than simply strong feelings about how you should slice bread. Is that why you came here? To get away from her?'

He laughed. 'That, and I have no citizenship in the place I've lived my entire life. My family moved to Singapore for my dad's job, but I no longer have any legal right to stay. Also, it's nice to be here and pretend I'm British, even though nothing here really makes sense. I can't believe you're all perfectly content to live in filth. The cities stink. The other day I saw a woman tip the entire contents of her black bin onto the street, for seemingly no reason at all.'

I looked at him and wondered if he'd grown up in the kind of place that had en-suite bathrooms and a fridge that dispensed ice.

'I know you think I'm a snob.' He absent-mindedly wiped away the scraps of candle wax I'd accumulated on the table. It was true he always looked neat and seemed to walk into every situation as though it should be designed to his liking. But I didn't think this was snobbery. He just liked the idea things could be improved. He was careful with his attention.

'Maybe you're more British than you think,' I said.

'Maybe I just want things to be better. Otherwise, what's the point of anything?'

I couldn't think about it until the food arrived. Nothing could be solved on an empty stomach. He rapped on the table next to my hand.

'Come on,' he said, 'you can't be zen about everything. You know what I mean.'

'I don't want to think about bin juice before the food arrives. But yes, English cities are disgusting in their own particular way.'

His finger grazed mine as he slid his hand away. 'Okay,' he said, 'we can talk about the bin stench after the pancakes. We can talk about your sister, too, if you like. Whenever you like, in fact.'

'This is why you're a writer, isn't it? You're endlessly interested by nothing at all.'

'Not nothing, Alice. Waste management is the very foundation of a functioning society.' He smiled at me, the little creases under his eyes deepening.

When the giant plate was placed in front of me, I realised Walt was right. The open crêpe with its golden lacey edges would do more to revive me than any book ever had.

He folded his up and ate greedily, without stopping. When he was done, he checked his phone, wiped the corners of his mouth and frowned. I was still slicing my own dinner into bite-sized portions, the cheese oozing out onto the plate. For a moment I chewed, watching him watch his screen. It was alienating and I wished he'd stop. Eating with someone required their full attention, because masticating at an empty shell of a person could make you feel particularly vulnerable and stupid.

'Everything okay?' I asked as he thumbed through a text.

He put his phone away.

'If you hurry up, we could probably make it back to the bookshop. Pretend like we'd been there the whole time.'

The restaurant smelt like butter and stodge. The kitchen sizzled behind us. I couldn't think of anything worse than going back and talking to a group of people. I put my knife and fork down as he looked over my shoulder to try and catch someone's attention.

'I think I'll just go back to halls, actually,' I said. Although many of us stayed off campus, Walt lived in the adjacent building to me.

He turned back to me. 'Ah. Time to catch up with the *boyfriend*?'

It was true that for a moment I wished my boyfriend didn't exist. Wouldn't it be easier to go back with Walt to the bookshop and forget about my old life, the one that was starting to feel more distant and surreal than the imaginary worlds I wrote about every day?

The first time my boyfriend read my writing, he asked if I was sad. I wondered how he'd extrapolated sadness from simply putting words to ordinary human feelings. My work was sad, I explained, but it was the doing it that made me happy.

'Like squeezing a spot?' he said.

I decided this was why writers always spoke about having an idea for a novel when no work ever materialised. I never questioned his own logic of doing self-indulgent things, like cooking baked potatoes with pasta and piling it all on a plate for me in a gesture of goodwill. I liked eating with him because he was like a Labrador that had just got into the bin. That was most of the fun of our relationship, a gluttony that went from plate to bed. But when I emailed him from my job at the council with little stories I'd written, he didn't know what to say. Very good, he'd often write, though you might have to explain it to me later.

I deleted those emails, embarrassed. I didn't want to explain anything. That was the whole point of writing it down.

When I left to start Sofie Muller's prestigious course, he stayed in his flat in Cambridge and I stopped sending him my writing. I had a whole classroom of people to tell me I was sad now.

I shook my head. 'He'll probably be out or asleep, anyway.'

'His loss.' The energy seemed to have drained from Walt. 'What are you going to do at nine o'clock on a Friday night in halls, then?' he said.

I thought about my small room and the bar of chocolate I'd left on my desk earlier in the day. I could finish binge-watching a home renovation show and forget I'd ever thought anything was more important than that.

'Write, I suppose,' I lied.

Two

Each week, we were given a different prompt to produce a piece of writing. Each week, Walt returned to his childhood: the blast of cold from shopping centres in high humidity, the taste of fresh orange juice from outdoor carts and learning to swim in water as hot as the air. Each week I tried to understand him through the lens he'd chosen, which I was starting to think was no way to understand anyone.

Our latest assignment was to pick a secret we hadn't told anyone else and turn it into a short piece of prose. Sometimes we were offered a newspaper clipping or an open-ended sentence to act as a prompt, but this time Sofie asked us to offer up our deepest thoughts.

She encouraged us to blur the line between truth and fiction as we took notes in thick, leather-bound pads. She paced round the room, fingering the elaborate clip that held her hair in place at the back of her head. The thing is, she told us, it was mostly easy for her to tell what's real and made up when we submit our work each week. 'The real trick is to make it difficult for me to work out which parts are from your own life and what you've pulled out from the freaky recesses of your mind.'

She walked around the classroom with the same quiet authority she'd had that first time I saw her at the bookshop. I imagined she carried this feeling everywhere she went, like a hot cup of tea inside of her that would never spill. Part of why we listened to her was to try and harness some of this for ourselves.

She put her coffee mug to her lips in thought. She brought this particular cup to every class we had. It was ceramic and looked homemade, with two protruding moulded breasts coming out of it. It was splattered with paint, one nipple pink and one purple, and the whole thing had a glossy glaze. Allegedly, it was cherished because it was a gift from a former student. We all wondered if the breasts were anatomically correct, and if so, who they belonged to.

It was so incongruous with the rest of her carefully crafted persona that the first time I saw it, it shocked me. It made me think that along with the small secret she herself might have about her own life, she might also be lewd and carnal and therefore, vulnerable even, like the rest of us.

When one of the other students, a middle-aged man called Henderson, pointed out we were taking a creative writing course, she waved his non-question out of the air with her hand. She sat on the desk, crossed her legs and pulled at the top of her suede boots, leaving a soft indentation from her fingers.

'Everything is fiction, all the time.' And, on the flipside, she could guarantee that we wouldn't be able to resist putting in all the mundanities of our own lives into our writing. It was part of the human condition that we think our own narrative endlessly interesting.

'So, we should only write what's true?' he said with a smirk. In moments like these, Sofie Muller held her own. She often baited us to underline her convictions. It was her fuel. If there was no one to pick a fight with, there was no way to win.

She smiled at no one in particular. 'Increasingly, I do believe you should only write what's actually happened to you, because everything else is bullshit. But,' she said, 'fiction is just about getting away with something. You have to be convincing. You have to convince me.' She put her mug down beside her. 'That's why I want your little secrets.' I kept my eyes fixed on her boots. The suede changed in the light so that when she put a toe forward it looked deepest darkest black, and when she retracted it, it faded to grey.

'You can decide what's true and what isn't,' she told us. 'But it's your job to make sure I can't tell the difference.'

I took everything she said incredibly seriously, and that was both my best and worst quality as a student.

In between classes, I worked for a luxury juice company that had a unit on an industrial estate nearby. Three times a week I would go to the unit and process their orders, emailing customers, printing out spreadsheets, labelling bottles and sliding them into silver, branded cool bags to be picked up by a courier. The juice was cold pressed from organic ingredients on big expensive machines that broke frequently. The kitchen was staffed exclusively by a group of women from Ukraine who were paid in cash like I was, but confided in me about wanting tax codes and payslips. I raised the issue with the American owner, Molly, who was younger than I was, but she only tucked her shiny hair behind her ear and said she was sorting it. The pay was impressively poor. One 250ml bottle would set us back the equivalent of an hour's wages.

The kitchen staff saw me as a vital link to Molly, a mouthpiece for their complaints that they worked too long hours and often ran out of spinach. During busy periods, I helped out in the kitchen and learnt to use the clunking juice machines, my hair in a net. Sometimes they worked for twenty hours straight when there was an event that required large quantities of kale and apple juice to be shipped off. I also regularly worked late into the night, compiling orders and sorting deliveries and invoices. Molly said her kitchen team were rock stars, but she never materialised for any great length of time. When she did, it was only to collect her own juices, of which she drank several litres a day, and to tell me it was okay if we ran out of fresh ingredients, as in a pinch the new juice could be topped up with the stuff that was five days old.

The first time I met Molly was in a café in town. She ordered us two overpriced pastries and then proceeded to tell me she never ate like this because she was vegan. I watched as she peeled apart her cinnamon bun strip by laminated strip, rolling each ribbon into a ball that she placed delicately in her mouth. I couldn't bring myself to eat it the same way, so took a large bite that left crumbs all over my jumper.

She'd asked me to bring some examples of blogs I'd written at university and for local publications. I'd quickly hurried together some pieces around organic produce and restaurant reviews that were half finished. I brought the blogs with me, printed out in a plastic wallet. I put them on the table in front of me when I arrived, sweating into my polyester blouse. She glanced at them and then asked me about my work ethic.

'It's obvious you're dedicated, Alice, because you write in your spare time.'

I wanted to say writing didn't always feel like work, but I let her imagine me slogging my guts out until midnight in front of a laptop. I told her about the KPIs I had to meet at the job I left before coming here. She said that was the kind of thing she was looking to implement in her business: processes and efficiency. The way she talked about juice made me want to curl up into a ball, but I needed the money and she was offering flexible hours at just above the minimum wage.

I asked her about the company and how she'd started it. I wanted to know what possessed someone who clearly came from money to start something that appeared to be largely unnecessary.

'When I started drinking cold-pressed juice, I felt like a different person. I wanted everyone to feel that way.' She dropped her bun on its plate and took a sip of lemon water as though this balanced it out. 'And now they can,' she said.

'That makes sense.' I leaned forward, ready to take another bite of my pastry. 'I suppose most people want to feel like a different person, and why wouldn't it be juice that'd do it?'

She eyed me as though she wasn't sure if I was mocking her.

'You can drink as much juice as you want if you work for me. You'll feel better, I promise.' I hadn't said I felt bad in the first place.

In the first few weeks, it became clear that Molly was never at the kitchen. I did, however, have to listen to her disembodied voice tell me about orders and produce emergencies on the phone at regular intervals. I never thought that carrots could be so nerve-inducing, but everything was chaotic and urgent. I painstakingly hand-wrote best before dates at ten o'clock at night when the sticker gun broke. I spent hours packing bottle after bottle into boxes, and never had more than two days off in a row.

But it was the distraction I needed from the parts of my life that were ruminative and solipsistic. The best part of my day was blending almonds and water and draining the mixture through a cheesecloth, watching the foamy milk settle into something wholly convincing.

Away from a screen, I was happy. I cut through the centre of vanilla pods and scraped their entrails into the mixture and realised that I'd never actually held or cut into a vanilla pod before. The black centre was engrossing and beautiful. As I wrapped a hand around the cheesecloth bundle of crumbly almonds, all trace of moisture drained away, I felt like I could stay interested in my work for hours.

The making, however, was only something I helped out with when everyone else was busy. Most of the time I was expected to be at my laptop negotiating bulk prices for cashew nuts and checking postcodes on the Royal Mail website. I never told Molly that all I wanted to do was make the milk and she never asked.

The woman who ran the juice production, Olena, was a couple of years older than me and spoke excellent English. She was always at the kitchen late at night, as the only woman trusted to mix the juice concoctions and fill the individual 250ml bottles to Molly's exact specifications. I was always there late on my shifts, too, as the juices went out to be delivered in time for people to start their cleanses the next morning.

When Olena finished her mixing, and I had packed the orders and booked the courier, we often sat together at the back of the kitchen in a partitioned office. One of the first nights we did this, she mentioned she had a husband and I told her she seemed young to be married.

She snorted. 'Maybe here I'm young, but somewhere else,' she gestured around her, 'I could be old.' She'd made us up a batch of fresh lemonade with a hint of cayenne pepper. Molly told us it was good for our digestion, but Olena said it was the only juice she could tolerate, probably because it was full of sugar.

'You don't have to wait with me for the couriers to come,' I told her. 'I'm happy to lock up on my own. There are always other people around on the estate.'

'I don't have anything better to do,' she replied, 'and I like the peace and quiet after a long day.'

I drained my juice and let the bitter dregs wash over my teeth.

'Don't you want to get back to your husband?'

She'd already worked twelve hours that day and was scrolling slowly on her phone sitting at the table with me, her back against the wall.

'Do you have a boyfriend?' she asked me.

'Yes, but I live at the university now, so I don't see him very much.'

She put down her phone and took a sip of her juice and then made a face.

'Your boyfriend, would you like to marry him?'

I considered this.

'Maybe one day. But I don't know.'

'It's best not to rush,' she said. 'I got married at nineteen and have never loved my husband. But my parents decided who I would marry, and I had to agree. Then, he decided he was going to England and I had to go with him. I was so sad.'

I asked if she missed her family and she said she did, very much. 'After ten years, we still don't love each other and now all everyone asks is why we don't have children.'

'Have you ever thought about getting a divorce?'

'I can't,' she said. 'My family are very religious so I would never be able to. But we won't ever have children because we no longer have a romantic relationship, if you understand my meaning. I have a friend I talk to, an English man, who is nice to me and wishes to be my boyfriend. I cannot date him, of course, but I enjoy his company.'

She took another phone out of her pocket. It was an old model that had physical keys and a small screen.

'I leave this one here,' she said. 'I use this phone to talk to my friend after everyone has left. Sometimes I stay for hours after I was meant to go home, just to text or call him.'

'Does your husband look at your main phone, then?' I asked her.

'Of course.'

'What do you like about your friend? Is he different from your husband?'

'He makes me laugh. He's nice to me, even though I don't sleep with him. He's still kind and wants to talk to me.'

Her rounded cheekbones gave her the appearance of a much younger woman, and even after a full day of work, her hair pulled up into a net, she was strikingly pretty. I wanted to tell her that if she did get a divorce, I'm sure she would find someone else, like this man, to start a new life with. That she wouldn't be on her own. But when she talked about her husband, she wore an amused, resigned expression for me: I would never understand. And when she talked, I nodded back at her: it was true, I wouldn't.

I still found the way she cherished that old phone waiting for her not-quite-lover's replies heartbreaking.

'I guess you'd like a romantic relationship with this man, but you can't have one,' I said.

She shook her head.

'But I know he wants one.' She looked at me with a deep seriousness. 'Sometimes he goes too far, but I know he's a kind man.'

I checked the time to see when the courier would be arriving. As the sky grew dark outside, I longed to be out of the kitchen, which always smelt like apples and cleaning fluid, and back in my own bed surrounded by the comfort of my solitude.

'We met up last week,' she said, putting her old phone back in her pocket as though her friend might be listening. 'We went to a pub in the countryside. We had a drink and he tried to kiss me and I told him no.'

'That must have been hard for you.'

'Yes, but he knows I am married. I've told him no many times. This doesn't stop him though, and he tells me that he believes one day we will be married instead. He thinks about me all the time and he knows we can't be together yet, but he said he wanted something from me so he could think about me even more.'

She looked up at me.

'Surely, you can already guess what he was asking for. Is this something English men often request or is it unusual?'

I shook my head, not understanding. I could tell she was embarrassed because her ears had flushed pink. I was overwhelmed in that moment by her sweet face and how forthcoming she was with information about her life to me, practically a stranger. I felt an urge to protect her.

'What did he want?'

'My underwear,' she said.

'Oh,' I said. 'Well, that isn't particularly strange, but if you feel uncomfortable with it, you shouldn't do it.'

She was visibly relieved that I hadn't expressed shock or horror.

'I said no, but he kept asking, pleading with me, again and again.

He wanted me to go to the toilet and take them off and give them to him.'

I nodded but didn't say anything.

'I didn't let him kiss me, not once,' she said.

'It doesn't matter to me whether you did or didn't.' I couldn't tell if she appreciated this or found it morally questionable.

'In the end I wanted to do it for him, because he's been so kind to me. I went to the ladies' bathroom and put my underwear in my coat pocket. I actually felt quite excited when I gave them to him, but I was wearing a dress and was terrified that as soon as we went outside, the wind would show everything to the world.' She smiled bashfully. 'We stood outside the toilets, and it wasn't even far from the bar, anyone could've walked by. He put his hand up my dress and I didn't stop him, even though we had never even kissed before. It sounds terrible,' she said, 'but I liked it. It was just for a minute and then he drove me home. That's all.'

'It's not terrible,' I said. 'It seems as though you really like this man and want to be with him – it's a shame you're with your husband who you don't feel romantic towards at all. It's all backwards!'

She agreed. 'Do you do these things with your boyfriend, Alice? Does he make you crazy?'

I was about to explain that he made me crazy, but mainly because he was always saying the wrong thing, when my phone started to buzz. The courier was here. When Olena helped me take the cool bags out to the van in front of the unit, the cold air hit me in the face and I felt strange, suddenly, to be possessed with knowledge of her inner life.

When the courier had gone, Olena asked if I was going home now to study and read books. I hugged her goodbye.

'Yes,' I said, 'and you should go home too, even if you don't really want to.'

'I never really want to,' she said, emphasising the 'really' as though imitating me, and laughed. 'Was it okay,' she said, 'to tell you that?'

I said it was okay and I wouldn't tell anyone if that's what she was worried about. She said that was good and then thrust a litre bottle of juice in my hand, 'because you like the beetroot and we have to throw it out soon anyway. And if you drink it all, don't worry when your pee turns pink.'

When I got back to my dorm room, the whole corridor was asleep. I had a shower and tried to wash the fruit smell off me. I lay down on my bed looking up at my books, thinking about Olena's assumption that I would spend the rest of the evening reading and studying. I thought of her in the pub, secretly delighted that a man who wasn't her husband wanted her underwear, and the feel of her bare skin against her dress. I thought about him pleading with her, again and again, until she relented. I thought about them standing in the hallway, his begging, telling her how much he wanted her, and feeling her arousal, telling her she was so wet, pushing her up against the wall where anyone could have walked by, and stroking her until she came. I touched myself.

When I was done, I opened up my laptop and decided to turn it into a story that would also be a secret.

Posted by aw0mbofonesown

Update: AITA for telling my male friends their stories of sexual harassment don't count?

Okay, that kind of blew up and not in a good way. Turns out, maybe I was the asshole. As suggested, I decided to talk to him more about his university tutor and not just dismiss his experience.

He said that it started months before she invited him round and assaulted him. First, she emailed him about books, then she encouraged him to share work with her in between classes. She told him that she loved working with him and that he was really talented. In the end, he struggled to create a healthy boundary between them. It all deteriorated pretty quickly after she made a move.

This was a few years ago now, but it turns out it's why he eventually dropped out of the course. I keep urging him to report it, even though it was a while ago. He also won't tell me who she is, but I can guess. She's kind of a big deal (and it's an open secret that she gets close to her students).

What is an open secret anyway? Something that everyone talks about but is too scared to do anything about? It's made me think this whole situation is much bigger than just what happened to him. So yes, I might have been the asshole originally, but really, she's the asshole. This whole situation is fucked.

925 comments

Three

Walt told me that when he first arrived in Norwich, he'd thought about paying for a short story online. That's the kind of thing you could do now, quite easily, he said. No one would ever know because it was just a simple transaction. He wanted his pieces to be good, and sometimes he couldn't trust his own writing. Sometimes it was easier not to get inside your own head and mine your own childhood trauma. He didn't always want to pick at an old festering wound and that was all writing was, some days. It wasn't cathartic like people said. It felt like raising the dead. 'Because that's what Sofie wants us to do in her class,' he told me. 'Find the wound and pick, pick, pick.'

Our hard deadline for each assignment was nine o'clock on a Sunday, and afterwards, those of us on campus would end up at the pub. One Sunday in our first term, he sat beside me with a pale ale, bemoaning Sofie's latest 'secret' prompt and the lack of inspiration it had elicited. He wanted to keep writing about growing up in Singapore, but he said there was something shameful about a childhood abroad. 'My mum likes to drink.' He paused, took a sip of his beer. I liked the way he was unfazed talking about his family. 'It's the combination of claustrophobic heat and having nothing to do. There's something kind of embarrassing about the whole thing. That, and the fact that we had a maid who refused a bed and slept on the kitchen counter.'

I listened to him talk in that alien way about England, a place he knew he was from but had never lived in until now. He went to an international school in Singapore, did his undergraduate degree in the US and now he was here, begrudgingly. I thought it must be a strange way to get to know the place you are from, by ending up in the flatlands of Britain's east coast writing about a childhood elsewhere.

'I miss the heat already,' he said, 'and I feel foreign even though I'm half-English and half supposed to be here.'

I nodded and sipped on my white wine, which was already warm. 'I've only moved about an hour from where I grew up in Cambridge,' I said, 'so the whole thing sounds incredibly exotic.'

He laughed. 'I find the Norfolk landscape monotonous,' he said, and I wondered how undulating Singapore could really be if you didn't count the skyscrapers. As far as I knew, it was full of golf courses, glass hotels and clean, chewing-gum-free streets.

'As soon as you come off the motorway you can see for miles in one straight line,' he said. 'It's incredibly dull to know exactly where you're going all the time, and for the place that you're going to not be any better than where you've come from.'

He made a fair point, but it was easier to get lost or stuck in a place like this than you'd think.

'Norfolk has the highest rate of incest in the country,' I said.

'Because it's so flat?'

I thought about it. 'I'm not saying one thing has anything to do with the other, but I'm not saying it doesn't. There's nothing else to do here anyway, which is probably grounds for doing something disturbing more often than you'd think.'

There was nothing else to do but write. That had been the last straw, I realised, for signing up to the course. For once it seemed timely and appropriate to do the obvious thing. I tapped the base of my wine glass and wondered when I should turn round and talk to another classmate. But there was something about Walt that always kept my attention. He could make the most mundane ideas entirely engrossing, simply by vocalising what other people didn't bother to say out loud. He would turn to me, waiting for my opinion, watching over the silence that hung between us so that I could have my say and so that he could respond to it.

What I mean is, it felt as though he deliberately left a gap he wanted me to fill, even if it was only about something stupid. It made me realise how often people talked without ever needing a response bigger than confirmation of their own ideas; without listening to a word from anyone else.

'I never thought I'd miss Singapore, you know. It never felt like home. I couldn't wait to leave,' he said. 'Now I miss it like a great hole in my heart, which is why I end up writing about it all the time. The piece I wrote to get a place on the course was about the class structure there and the strange social mores I witnessed with great confusion as a child. But the trick is to let yourself miss somewhere without indulging it.'

'What do you mean?' I said.

'Every time I forget some small detail and go to call my mother for one of my pieces – like the name of the swimming club she took me to every Saturday as a child – the illusion is shattered. When she answers the phone, I know I don't miss anything about it. All I can remember is her having fights with the neighbour downstairs about the noise of the air conditioning.' He sighed. 'In my idealised memory, I only hear the soft click of Mahjong tiles and know I was happy, but I don't think I was ever happy there, not even as a child, not even once.'

'Everyone is happy once,' I said, picking at a wet beer mat without looking at him. 'Even a stopped clock is right twice a day.' I had a strange desire for him to say he was happy now, in Norfolk, in this pub – with me.

'I suppose I was always happy to take a shit.' He took a large swig from his drink. 'But it rarely happened twice a day.' He laughed then. 'Okay,' he said, 'why don't you tell me all the particular ways your childhood was happy, when your sister wasn't acting up. What was it like to really love your parents, even if they were largely boring, and feel nostalgic for a crinkling paper bag of hot, salty chips after a day together playing amicably on an English beach?'

I was about to point out that I never said my childhood was an Enid Blyton novel, when Grace came to sit beside us. She was vocal in class, in a way I'd noted always captured Walt's attention. It was obvious he found her charming, which she was. Even though she was around my age, I felt like she'd figured something out that I hadn't. She had long, silky hair and a pretty face, but most of all she made people she liked feel endlessly interesting. It was a nice trick: she would put a hand on their arm, lean in and look them in the eyes. It took me a while to work out that she was the interesting one after all.

The intimacy we'd enjoyed vanished. Walt turned towards Grace, offering to top up her wine. He laughed at the story she told about her interview for the course.

'She gave me a photocopy from one of her own novels,' Grace said, 'and asked me what I thought about it. I fumbled around the issue, complimenting the piece wildly, before realising this was *Sofie Muller* – she wouldn't be impressed without an honest critique.'

'So, what did you do?' I held my hand flat against my wine glass, trying to cool the rising heat in my face from embarrassment by proxy.

'I told her it was a bit aloof,' she said. 'And I wanted to know more about the protagonist, who . . .' she elbowed Walt, '. . . is so obviously her. But of course, she didn't give anything away. I must have said something right because now I'm here drinking a five-pound glass of wine with you lot. I read something about it online,' she said. 'She likes to hear her words read aloud by her students.'

'Well, you can't be a famous novelist without being a bit

self-absorbed.' Walt picked up his beer mat and started tap-tap-tapping it on the table.

Grace shook her head. 'She wants us to suck her dick.'

We laughed, but Walt only sniffed, looking down at his beer. 'She's the kind of woman you want to please even when she tells you your work is shit,' he said. 'I'm telling you now.'

'So, you believe the rumours then?' said Grace.

He didn't miss a beat. 'The point is that everyone has heard them. So it's irrelevant whether they're true or not.'

She raised an eyebrow. 'I read online that she once had a threesome with two students in her swimming pool.'

I let out a breath of disbelief. 'Everyone's heard stories like that.' I lifted my glass up to my lips and then added: 'Everyone's heard stories like that about every successful woman.'

'Oh,' said Grace, 'it's not that I'm threatened by the idea that literary professors might be looking for love affairs.'

'It's kind of sad, rather than scandalous, when you think about it,' Walt said. 'Maybe she's just lonely.'

Grace looked surprised. She briefly touched him on the arm, and he lifted his head towards her. A tiny crest of beer foam rested on the facial hair above his lip. I watched the two of them, wondering if she might lift a delicate finger to wipe it off. 'Bit of a soft spot for an older woman?'

He smiled at her and then ran a hand over his mouth, whether because he felt self-conscious or he sensed the moisture, I wasn't sure. 'Just a soft spot for women, generally.'

'Ah,' she said, 'completely indiscriminate then.'

'Completely.'

She looked away from him and laughed. My stomach lurched.

'I think we should be more worried about her feedback than who she is or isn't sleeping with,' I said. What was also talked about online were her ritual workshop humiliations. No one was ever left unscathed.

'It's what we signed up for,' Grace said. 'When I thought about the year ahead I prepared myself for an onslaught of critique so great that I might never want to pick up a pen again. I heard that was what writing courses were all about, whether your tutor was Sofie Muller or someone a little less intimidating. Either way, it's time to grow a thick skin, and fast.'

Walt picked up my beer mat now and took on the task of ripping it up. Clearly Grace's warning had taken the glee out of the conversation for him.

'I'll be lucky if I manage to write anything at all,' he moaned.

'Oh, and another thing!' Grace slammed a hand down on the table and the rest of the group looked around at her. She smiled at them apologetically, but her voice became more animated with the increased audience. 'She opened a Coke Zero at the end of the interview with a spoon,' she nodded conspiratorially. 'So as not to break a nail.' A real power move, she assured us.

I went back to my room and called my boyfriend. 'I don't know why I feel sort of in awe of Sofie, but obviously if anyone's going to know how to write a novel it's someone who's actually done it,' I said. 'Not everyone on the course feels that way, and in fact for some people it's a reason to disregard everything she says. They think she's got her own agenda and rigid style. And that she just wants to get us drunk and use us for attention.' I listened to the silence down the line. 'You're not saying anything.'

'I'm nodding,' he said.

'Do you like older women?'

He breathed out. 'Alice,' he said, 'I like *you*.'

'I miss you. I miss being with you. I miss feeling normal.' I was sitting cross-legged on my bed, squeezing a pillow in one hand and holding the phone in the other.

'Why don't you feel normal?'

I wanted to push my face into the pillow and breathe in the smell of night-time. 'I spend all day trapped in an imaginary world, only to be told in class I've got it wrong, actually. The world I've created from nothing, in my head, should be a bit more like this.'

'Well maybe you should try what she said. Try and tell the truth.'

'The truth is boring.' The truth was I liked someone else. There, I thought, now I can admit it. 'You're right,' I said. 'Maybe I need to be more honest with myself in my writing.' In my head I reasoned that I could write about anything and he'd never read it anyway. 'I don't know, what do you think?'

He told me he was boiling potatoes and they were almost done.

'What are you having for dinner?'

'Potatoes,' he said.

I told him I had to go, someone was knocking at the door. After I hung up, I looked at the David Foster Wallace novel I'd bought after getting onto the course but hadn't yet read. It was weighty in my hands and I willed it to tell me the secret to all books. I put it back and marvelled at its wide spine amongst all the other spines, some cracked, most not. I thought about all the books I'd never get round to. I trailed my fingers over them, tapping each one in turn. This was part of reading, I decided, the thinking about it. The marvelling was just as important as the doing. I could have read three chapters in the time I sat and looked at them, thinking about doing it. It was all part of the work. That was the kind of thing Sofie Muller would say. It was all part of the work.

Four

After we handed in our latest assignment, Sofie asked us all to come for drinks at her house. It was before we were due to workshop our stories, and the group developed a prurient interest in each other's secrets as we read the pieces online. There it was in black and white: Henderson's loveless marriage; Stella's stint at rehab; Grace's body issues.

We drank cans of gin and tonic on the train to Sofie's remote village. Walt downed his quickly, as though he had social anxiety. He crushed the can in an elaborate gesture before turning to me and saying he thought what I wrote about my boyfriend was very brave.

'What made you think it was about my boyfriend?'

He looked down at my hand gripping my own drink and I glanced at Stella and Grace laughing together opposite us, wondering if they were listening.

'I just assumed it was a recent incident,' he said. 'I think it's layered with a lot of literary merit.'

In the piece, my protagonist writes in her diary that one night, at a pub, a man who isn't her boyfriend asks her to take off her underwear and give it to him – she complies. I tried to contain a thrill from his misguided assumption.

'You don't have to sound so surprised. Did you not expect me to be able to write?'

'It's always the quiet ones that sneak up on you. You're very talented.' He paused. 'Maybe I just wanted it to be about you. Maybe I just hoped things with your boyfriend weren't that great.'

I didn't say anything.

'Sorry,' he said. 'You know what I mean.'

'Who's to say it's my secret, anyway?'

He shook his head. 'Regardless, I thought it was a great piece.'

I wondered if we'd always be so considerate to each other or whether in class the compliments would soon deteriorate into constructive criticism about run-on sentences.

When we arrived at the station, we took a couple of taxis down winding country lanes and ended up in front of large industrial-looking gates.

'Someone has to buzz the buzzer,' Stella whispered as she pressed into me from the window seat.

Walt told everyone not to worry, Sofie had emailed over the code. He jumped out and pressed it into the pad. The gates jolted and then opened onto a small drive leading up to a Modernist home. It was long and squat, but made up of intentionally eroded materials to give a soft bronze patina to the outside walls. Spotlights lit up the wide windows all along the building. I'd heard there was a swimming lake and five acres of land out the back, along with a corrugated iron writing shed with art deco furniture. A double-width front door opened and Sofie appeared wearing what appeared to be expensive silk pyjamas.

Walt nudged me in the ribs. I knew he thought it was trivial to care about clothes when there was work to be done. But there was Sofie Muller, standing in her doorway like something I used to pore over in a magazine: her hair teased up on her head in smooth waves, a matching scarf tucked neatly behind her ears. A long hand propping open the door and a small, contained smile that betrayed pride in her house.

In the kitchen, snacks and drinks littered a huge marble island that overlooked a wall of glass. I tried to squint through the growing darkness outside to see if I could spot the swimming lake or writing shed, but Stella tapped my shoulder and gave me a goblet filled with gin and tonic. When Sofie was out of earshot, she said: 'Is it gauche to ask for the whole house tour?'

'Maybe if we had one, we'd find the room she actually lives in. You know, the one with the piles of books and lumps of chewing gum and screwed up pieces of paper.' I looked around. 'Houses that are too clean make me suspicious.'

We walked around and spotted objects of interest that we'd discuss at great length when we were next alone: photographs of Sofie with various beautiful men; a Gucci cocktail glass; a calendar on the fridge; a framed print of the cover of her first novel.

I stuck doggedly to my one empty glass of gin for hours, only putting it down when I went in search of the toilet. I rattled the handle of the downstairs bathroom, but it appeared to be locked. I looked up the stairs to the unlit landing and decided that I couldn't wait. I took off my shoes and padded slowly upwards, looking back over my shoulder a couple of times as I did so.

There were several rooms leading off the landing, but only one door open, where a lamp was lit. I went towards it and pushed it open slowly. It was a bedroom, but I couldn't tell if it was Sofie's or a guest room. It betrayed no signs of the personalisation we insisted upon at university: guitars propped against the wall, literary posters, piles of books. Even the bedside table had only a blown glass lamp and one book that showed no indication of having been careworn. The bed was neatly made in a pink linen set and the walls were painted a dark colour, almost black. It was a cosy room, but it wasn't homely. I curled my toes into the plush rug at the foot of the bed. A Japanese antique print hung above the headboard; a velvet green throw had been folded neatly over the duvet.

I wanted to find something weird, repulsive even. I wanted to know something about Sofie I couldn't read online. A piece of hard skin on the carpet, a packet of pills for some private inflammation, an enigmatic sex toy hidden in a drawer, a small blood stain on a sheet, a clump of hair discarded in the toilet. Instead, I stood there, my arms folded, staring at the swirling pattern of the blue glass lamp and, I suppose, waiting for someone to find me. If Sofie came in the room, it'd be the kind of thing she always thought of when she saw me in class. She'd wonder if I opened that drawer on her bedside table, if I touched the brass handle between my fingers and looked at what was inside and laughed at her.

I heard a creak on the landing and instantly regretted being there. My shoes were placed together at the foot of the stairs like a giant symbol of guilt. I looked around; there was another door in the bedroom that led onto what looked like an en suite. I went in quietly and shut the door. I still needed the toilet, but now I was too afraid to go in case she was coming up to look for me. But it was also my alibi, so I turned on the light and sat down on the toilet in front of me, trying to slow my breathing and listen to what was outside. A laugh from downstairs, the distant hum of music. Footsteps, confident and plodding, getting louder.

I looked around. The bathroom was white and clean, made up of the same marble as the kitchen. There was an open shower and a claw-footed bath. But here – I looked at the back of the door – a purple silk robe hung up, creased on the sleeves. And on the sink, a balled-up tissue and a bottle of Jo Malone. Oh God, I thought, it *is* her bathroom. I was sitting on the toilet in Sofie Muller's bathroom. Then – a knock at the door.

I cleared my throat but didn't say anything. I waited. I opened my mouth and closed it again. Another knock. I pulled down my tights hurriedly and used all my concentration to force out a trickle of wee. I grabbed some toilet roll and then flushed, throwing the balled-up tissue in there as well, and pulled up my tights with such force that a ladder appeared on my thigh.

I waited for another knock but there wasn't one. I brushed my hands over my skirt and walked towards the door as if it were perfectly obvious I was in here because I was meant to be. I opened the door and threw my head back, then let out a little yelp: Walt.

He made an elaborate gesture of moving out of the doorway with a small smile.

'Alice, what are you doing in here?' He looked behind me inside the bathroom and then over his shoulder.

'Having a piss – what are *you* doing in here?' I said in what I imagined to be a very nonchalant manner.

He huffed and looked around again nervously, muttering that he was there to find me, obviously.

I laughed. 'Do you think if I snapped a pic it'd go viral?' I said, pointing at the bed.

'Maybe if it was her actual bed or her lingerie or something.'

'How do you know it isn't?' I said.

I showed him the back of the door. 'I found her robe, though.' I reached out a hand to touch its silky material and Walt said my name sharply. I jumped, letting my hand drop to my side.

'Oh, relax, Whitman. It's just a joke.'

He smiled at the new nickname, but then stepped towards me cautiously. 'I don't like this, let's go back downstairs.'

There was something about his nervousness that I enjoyed. It was one of the first times I'd seen him vulnerable and not casually self-assured. I was close enough to see the stubble on his face and a light flush on his cheeks. I realised I had his whole attention.

'Worried she might fail you for stepping foot upstairs?' I teased.

'It's just weird. I'm going.' He turned to move back towards the stairs and I grabbed the edge of his T-shirt. The fabric pulled towards me and exposed a slice of skin above his hip. I glanced down reflexively and then let go. 'Don't go,' I said.

He looked back at me, a slight smile appearing at the edges of his mouth. 'Alice,' he said. I wanted him to kiss me, and feared it too, feared what it would set in motion. But I had to know that he really wanted to put his mouth on mine, even if it didn't happen. The step forward, the desire to act, was the most important part.

He lifted a hand to my face, as though it was the most natural thing in the world, and put his lips on mine. I didn't stop him like I thought I might. I wanted him so much. His mouth opened slightly, asking a question of me. I kissed him back, my hand stroking the short hair at the back of his neck. He leaned into me with a confidence that appeared out of nowhere.

I could smell the perfume from Sofie's bathroom. He pushed me gently until my back was against the doorjamb.

He put a hand on my skirt. 'Did it happen like this, in your story?'

It would have been so easy to pull him into the bathroom and tell him to touch me, up against Sofie Muller's sink. I could pull the anecdote out at parties in ten years' time. But I didn't want him to want me because of something I'd made up. I pushed gently on his chest. 'Let's not,' I said.

'I thought you were into it.' He pulled away.

I laughed and told him that he needn't have come all the way up here to find me. I would do perfectly well to find my own way back down.

'There's no need to become Elizabeth Bennet.' Then he shook his head and smiled. 'You're a strange person.'

'I'm the worst.'

'Is this about your *boyfriend*?' He said the word in a childish sing-song.

'Right. Maybe.'

'You lost focus for a second, didn't you?'

Yes, he was a nice distraction. 'I'll concentrate harder next time.' I wiped my mouth with my hand and we went back downstairs.

* * *

Sofie used to make us read aloud from her books in class. She would grunt, folding one long-booted leg over the other if we mispronounced a word. My eyes would dash forward on the photocopied pages to see which passage would be mine and then I would fret endlessly about it until she said my name – and then I would begin.

What I'm saying is: she scared me. She scared all of us.

Even as I watched her on her sofa late that evening, she still scared me, her legs outstretched on the coffee table and her headscarf lying on the floor, hair curling around her forehead. She looked even more beautiful in disarray.

A woman from our class, Beatrice, was talking and gesticulating next to her, while Henderson was sitting on a chair opposite them, tapping his glass but saying little. I wandered over and reminded them that we had taxis booked at 11 to take us back to the station for the last train. Sofie patted the sofa cushion on the other side of her.

'I'm telling them about the time I was going to go to Venice with David Hockney,' she said. 'I never made it, because I'd bought some new shoes that were incredibly high and slipped down my front steps that morning. I had to go to the hospital.' She paused between each sentence, unafraid of the silent gaps she left. 'That's how my partner at the time found out my real age.'

I snorted and tried to remember if I'd ever read this anecdote in a novel. I sat down beside her and got a hit of her perfume.

She'd been so pleased with the shoes, she said, and it had all turned out horribly. It happened after her third book took off and she started getting invited to exotic places with interesting people. 'But then I ended up in hospital, the worst kind of place, with someone who couldn't believe I was really that ancient. The waffle blanket and plaster cast didn't help. It made no difference before so it shouldn't have made any difference then.' She looked at me, tucking a piece of hair behind her ear. 'I suppose people don't lie about these things now.'

I wondered if I should answer. Beatrice giggled.

'It's a bit of a defence mechanism isn't it, lying about stupid things?' Sofie continued. 'When I was at school, there was a group of girls that bullied me. After that, sometimes it felt better to lie and live in a dreamworld.'

Beatrice said eagerly, 'Yes, little lies can be a safe haven from the crushing melancholy of reality.' She was sitting slightly too close to Sofie, her knees pressed forward against hers.

Ignoring her, Sofie turned towards me, her arm across the back of the sofa. 'You know how I got back at them? I gave them a nickname and it made me feel better. It's silly, isn't it, the things you do when you're young.' She leaned forward and put her drink down on the coffee table, suddenly serious. Then she plunged her fingers into her glass and gripped an olive, shaking it gently before popping it into her mouth, her tongue extended. 'I thought your latest piece was very clever,' she said. I moved my hair away from my face, stunned into grateful silence.

Beatrice cut in. 'Do you think you're an architect or a gardener?' Sofie didn't say anything. 'You know, in your head at least.'

'We can be whatever we want in our own heads.' Sofie gestured towards an empty snack platter on the coffee table. 'You can always count on writers to be hungry.'

I hadn't touched a single piece of food, fearing that I'd make some social error and drop it down my top. But she was right, I was absolutely starving.

Beatrice tried again. 'Do you write by hand?'

Sofie didn't answer, but Henderson perked up. 'Even in the few weeks I've been here,' he said, 'I've gone back to handwriting and feel like I've been given back a real gift. Because you lose the ability to write by hand well very quickly. You have to re-train your fingers not to seize up. I used to be so good at it, all those hours of law exams where we had to write everything by hand. The real exam wasn't even about what you'd learnt or could remember, or even what you were really writing. It was just about handwriting, and how much you could get down legibly on paper.'

None of us replied to him, but with the confidence of a middle-aged man, he continued: 'But I was good at it. The pages would crinkle under the weight of my biro, and even the smell of it was satisfying. I live in fear of the delete button. You know, that you tap-tap-tap and one wrong click and there's nothing left of it. There's something reassuring about a notebook. I think writing by hand is a small effort against the gamification of everything we do, even if my wife often tells me how pointless it is.'

I looked at the skin under his eyes, slightly drooping and folded. I could imagine him as a child, his delight at slapping his exam paper shut, his ink-stained fingers. I wanted to tell him I knew what he meant, but the only handwritten work I treasured were childhood diaries, and they had all been about sorrow and private pain.

Walt reappeared behind us in the kitchen and Henderson went over to join him in another drink. Sensing a pause in the conversation, Beatrice reluctantly got up. I sat smiling at Sofie stupidly. I was going to excuse myself and offer to refill her drink, but my hand moved involuntarily and I knocked her glass over on the coffee table. She pulled her legs up in one smooth motion and righted it. I apologised, but she patted my hand.

'It's fine, it was empty anyway.' From this close up, her cheeks looked soft, powdered. I could see where she'd filled in her eyebrows with small strokes. It gave something away. She wiped the table with her napkin. 'I guess we're all a little over-served tonight.'

I didn't tell her that although I seemed drunk, I was just nervous. I hadn't had more than one gin the entire night.

'Some a little more than others.' She winked at me. Then she patted my hand again and for a moment, left hers on top of mine. I retracted my hand like a reflex and apologised again, but she was already up and back in the kitchen, telling Walt to help himself to more olives.

I looked around and everyone seemed drunk. I wanted to go home. As though to redeem myself, I followed her to the kitchen. As I put my glass on the counter, I looked over at Walt, who was talking to Grace. I was too far away to hear what they were saying. One of his hands was in a bowl of crisps, the other grazed her waist. The touch was easy, comfortable, and she showed no sign of surprise. Just as he moved his hand off her, he looked at me. He smiled as though to say: *Yes, and?* as he shovelled crisps into his mouth.

I turned to Sofie. 'Those girls that taunted you at school. What did you call them? What was the nickname?'

'The Bitches of Eastwick,' she said, smiling. Even years later, I could see the pleasure it gave her to say the words out loud.

While I waited outside for the taxis to arrive, I looked back at Sofie's house and marvelled that I had just been inside. I called my boyfriend and told him that another man had just tried to kiss me.

'Oh,' he said cheerfully. 'Well, that's no good.'

'No, I know.' I looked around at the windows lit up in a wash of gold. 'It isn't.'

'I hope you told him to shove off.'

'Of course. I just thought I should tell you.'

'How's the writing going?'

'It's going.'

'Have you written about me yet?' He let himself have a little laugh.

'Not yet.'

'You're being very quiet.'

'I'm scared,' I said. 'I'm scared that this year has just begun and that soon it will already be over. I'll be back at my job at the council and back in my stupid little flat with mould and pointless furniture. I feel like I'll never feel good again until I've done something and ended up like someone, like Sofie Muller. Maybe it's okay to feel like that really strongly? Maybe it means I'll really do it, you know?'

He said there was nothing wrong with my little flat and not all the furniture was pointless. 'Do you remember that IKEA side table? It had that name we always laughed about.'

'I can't remember the name. I left it at the recycling centre when I left.'

I heard an exhale.

'Maybe it's not the furniture that's pointless. Maybe it's me,' I said. He didn't say anything. I put my free hand in my coat pocket. I wanted to go upstairs and lie in Sofie Muller's pink sheets. 'Everything just feels so much *less* pointless when I write it down.' The words came out like a whine.

'So, it's good. The reason you're there, it's a good thing.' This was his way of telling me not to complain. 'I thought you weren't that bothered about being published anyway? Isn't that what you're always saying? It's about the process, or something.'

'Or something.'

He paused and let out a frustrated sigh. I could hear the click of a mug landing on his kitchen counter. 'LACK,' he said. 'That little table was called LACK.'

Posted by aw0mbofonesown

Update: AITA for telling my male friends their stories of sexual harassment don't count?

Just wanted to let you know that my friend has now reported his experience about his female tutor to the university. I showed him all your responses and he was really overwhelmed, but I think it's helped him process a lot of stuff. Hey, that's the power of the internet.

He wanted to say thanks. To answer some of your questions, he had to provide his phone number and personal email when he joined the course, so I guess that's how she got those. There's actually no rule against that kind of communication at a university (not like the safeguarding that happens at school).

He said it was hard to call her out because she helped him with his writing, so it put him in an awkward position. In the end, he stopped reading, and he hasn't written anything for years. He's now a software developer and is doing really well, so he doesn't want you all to worry about him. He told me to tell you: It was just one of those unfortunate things that happened. At the end of the day, life is good. He told me this while drinking the first cold beer at the end of a long day and I feel like he meant it. Life is fine, he said.

1,038 comments

Five

Walt told me that if he was going to murder me, he'd bury my body by the lake.

He'd written a story for class that week where his character had clobbered his girlfriend over the head and then hidden her possessions in nearby spaces as red herrings. He'd buried her body in the woods and then kept hearing creaking outside his window, like the trees were angry. The character had started to believe the trees were out to get him because he had used them to help hide her body. The trees knew too much and had a way of communicating. They were in a conspiracy and the character knew it, so he spent the rest of the story trying to think of a way to hide her body away from the trees but still under cover. When he finally attempted to dig up her body, he became spooked by the sound of the wind and had tripped and fallen on an exposed root. He sprained his ankle and called out in pain, where he was promptly discovered by hikers.

Grace told him that she liked the idea of tree sabotage, and of them talking to each other, because don't they do it anyway through their root networks? But she did think the ending needed work. 'Isn't it a bit obvious for him to be discovered because of a tree? Wouldn't the hikers just find the woman's body anyway? Why do women always have to die?'

'The ending makes sense,' Walt said, 'because it was the character's own projected anthropomorphising of the trees that caused him to go back to the woods where they would be his downfall. I was trying to say that the things that have a hold over us are the things we give power to.'

'I didn't even think much about the trees at all,' Henderson said. 'I barely noticed the lengthy descriptions of bark and sodden leaves because I was too horrified by the description of the girl's death. Why did he have to smash her face in with the base of a wine bottle? It seemed slow and painful and too middle-class for words.'

'It was just the first thing that came into my head,' Walt admitted.

I had been struck by the bottle of wine too. The description of the bloodied glass and the final smash over her features, rendering her entirely unrecognisable. I asked him if he'd thought about how the character would have got all that blood out of his flat and what his motivation was to kill her in the first place. 'It seemed completely arbitrary. That one minute they were fine and the next he was angry because she asked him to turn down the volume on the telly.' I felt my face grow warm when I said this and he smiled at me. I was doing my best to pretend we hadn't kissed only a few days ago.

Sofie cut in. 'The scenes are meant to act as moments or chapters from a novel, not short stories. They don't have to be neat or complete, so don't worry about the wider context, just focus on what you're reading.' She was sitting at the front of the class, enraptured by Walt's story. It was up on the screen and she'd highlighted bits she'd enjoyed. She'd liked the bloodiness of it, but the tree torture had kept it literary.

'I agree,' I said. 'For me it never felt hammed-up or hyperbolic, because the mental anguish was so focused on the landscape and nothing else. It's sensory. It reminded me of *The Yellow Wallpaper*.' I looked over at Walt, who was nodding with a small smile on his face.

Next, we turned our constructive criticism to Henderson's piece. He'd written a story about a lawyer who hits on a younger female colleague, presuming she returns his affections. When he's turned down, he is so humiliated that he finds it difficult to return to work and spends several paragraphs swimming obsessively in his local pool. As a result, the character becomes fitter than he has been since he hit middle age.

No one in the class mentioned the fact that the character had the same job as Henderson. The long descriptions of longing for his colleague, as well as the shame of thinking a younger person would be interested in him, were so exquisitely detailed it was hard not to assume it came from personal experience.

Sofie took umbrage with his piece right away. As she flicked the story up onto the screen, it was littered with her favourite shorthand markings suggesting he'd repeated himself, used a cliché or droned on for too long. She pointed at one of her acronyms, UI (under-imagined), where she thought he'd used a well-worn phrase. This could easily tip over into T (trite). Another, DSIT (don't say it twice); was a favourite that cropped up a lot when marking our pieces. 'The reader gets that he's ashamed,' Sofie said, focusing on one paragraph. 'You don't need to tell us so five times. Leave a little for us to fill in the blanks.'

The fact that the story in some ways resembled Henderson's autobiography and was perhaps sharing his own secret shame didn't seem to make her go easy on him. If anything, it made her harder.

We were sitting at desks in a U-shape, and Sofie was in the centre. She was standing next to her laptop, projecting her screen and pacing with her ceramic breasts mug in hand. We were waiting for her to finish her overall feedback so we could get to our discussions. Henderson pretended to make notes as she pulled apart his 2,000 words. His thumb had turned blue from the fountain pen ink, and I remembered what he'd said about writing by hand as a student. He must have touched his mouth as he also had a tiny smudge on his lip.

He pointed at the projected image of his work. Throughout the piece, Sofie had included the letters OW at various points. He winced as though he was acting out the acronym. 'What does OW mean, again?'

'Overwrought,' Sofie said, matter-of-factly. 'I felt that some of your sentences were straining to be mournful.' She drummed her fingers on the projector, as though deep in thought, and then took a sip from her coffee. 'But they don't quite make it.'

I was desperate to tell Henderson that I had genuinely liked the piece, and it had been one of the few bits of writing from the week I'd been excited by. Whether that was because of the scandalous window into his own life or because of excellent writing, it didn't matter. I could feel his embarrassment from where I sat and wanted to tell him he was good. But I knew that the damage had been done.

It was hard to come back from withering summations from Sofie, even if you didn't agree with her. I often wondered if the idea was to make you work harder in your next piece, now all your writing tics had been publicly surfaced and removed, or whether it was simply a necessary humiliation because she didn't like your writing. Either way, at the end of that class I hated her. And more than ever, I was desperate for her approval.

Henderson cleared his throat but didn't say anything. Sofie moved on to discussing his inclusion of a dream sequence, something she felt worked against the purpose of good writing. She stared at the illuminated screen, littered with her own markings. 'The thing about dreams,' she mused, 'is that they're a bit like children. Yours are endlessly interesting, but when people start talking about their own . . . it's quite dull. There are exceptions – when it comes to dreams, not children – but unfortunately, this is not one of them. The structure feels disjointed, each section is a kind of incomplete scenelet.'

While we were all sitting in dumb silence, Grace spoke up. 'That's surely a stylistic choice,' she said, calmly. 'The short, sparse paragraphs make the whole thing more emotionally fraught. It came across to me as entirely deliberate.'

Sofie pressed her lips together as though she was contemplating the suggestion.

'Perhaps so, but over the course of a novel this wouldn't work, the style couldn't be sustained.' She looked at Henderson, who stared down at his fountain pen and notebook. 'And this is a novel writing course, after all.' She turned back to the screen to continue her feedback, but Grace carried on.

'I think you could definitely sustain it. It's just a different way of doing things, that's all. There's no one way to write a novel, is there, so why *couldn't* you write it like this?'

Sofie smiled and sat down on her desk, swinging one leg over the other. 'I suppose you could. But if you're going to write in a very sparse way, every word needs to carry a lot of weight. You're asking the quality of your prose to do some incredibly heavy lifting.' She tapped the top of her knee as though debating what to say next. 'In this instance, I didn't feel that the work quite held up under that scrutiny.'

I blinked, willing my mind to leave the room. I imagined my bedroom in halls, the shelves of books and the image of my laptop and notebook next to it, a biro discarded on the page. And my own coffee cup, the enormous kind that you get free from a sports shop. I knew it was there waiting for me. I knew in less than an hour, I'd be back home, safe. I just couldn't feel it.

'That's your opinion,' Grace said. She lifted her biro and pointed towards Sofie, as though it wasn't already obvious who she was talking to.

Sofie put her mug down with a click.

'Naturally, it is.'

As I waited for Grace to fill the silence, I glanced at Henderson, whose mouth hung slightly ajar. I could see a pearl of spit on his lower lip, glistening.

'In which case,' Grace lowered her biro and put her hands flat over her notebook. 'Maybe it would be interesting to hear what everyone else thought.' Sofie shrugged and offered us the palm of her hand as though to encourage conversation. We were all stunned into silence, trying not to look directly at Grace or Henderson. My eyes were fixed on the curve of the bodily outline on Sofie's mug, wishing I wasn't anywhere near this room.

'I thought it was brave,' Grace said finally. 'It turned a middle-class stereotype into a very empathetic figure.'

'*Did* you empathise with the character? Or pity him?' Sofie asked her.

'I empathised with him,' Grace shot back. 'That's why the structure worked. There was no room for saccharine writing. There was no room for pity.'

Sofie nodded at Henderson as though she was conceding he'd won this round. A few of us also added our thoughts to the discussion. We loved the bit with the dog. We thought it strange that he'd order pineapple in the restaurant. Did the kitchen table carry any weighty significance? There was something ominous about the windows. There was always something ominous about windows. And although we loved the bit with the dog, was it a sort of Chekhov's dog? Was the dog going to have to die, like his marriage?

Henderson responded diligently to our thoughts, but he shrunk down in his seat. I couldn't tell if he was grateful for what Grace had said. I couldn't help imagining him as a child at school, being told by a teacher that people felt sorry for him. I wanted the class to be over, so I doodled on my printout and said nothing.

As we got towards the end of the session, Sofie scrolled through her markings on Henderson's piece one more time. She tapped her pen against the side of her laptop as though something had just occurred to her. 'The scene where he's swum too far, for too long, and thinks he might choke on the chlorine-filled water.' Sofie pulled her pen up to her mouth, hovering it by her bottom lip.

'That felt real. I could feel the burning down his throat.' There was a notable exhale that went around the room. She went over to the wall and indicated the section she was referring to. She looked at Henderson, who was finally looking back at her. 'More like this,' she said.

Walt walked me back to my room after class for a cup of tea. I put the two mugs down on my desk. I asked him if he'd thought about the fact that after Christmas, we had to have a concrete premise for our novel that would become our dissertation. 'Do you think you'll do yours on the tree girl?'

He laughed and sat down next to me on the edge of my bed. 'I weirdly enjoyed writing it.'

I took a sip from my tea. 'You got off a lot lighter than Henderson.'

He nodded. 'The thing about this course, is that you realise you're both more and less special than you think. Or at least, that's how Sofie makes you feel.'

'I could tell you enjoyed writing it. It was so specific, like you'd thought about it a lot.'

'I guess I have. The story was just like one big intrusive thought.' I frowned and he smiled at me. 'Don't you ever get them? My character killed his girlfriend with a wine bottle, but it would make a lot more sense for me to kill you by poisoning your tea. You're always drinking the stuff and no one would guess, would they? Then I'd bury your body by the lake where the ground is really soft. Or weigh it down so you stayed at the bottom. You wouldn't believe the kind of shit they drag up from canals and ponds that no one has seen in decades.'

'I don't know why you'd poison me when you could so obviously overpower me physically. Wouldn't it be better just to strangle me and not leave any evidence behind at all? It should be me poisoning you. I'd put it in those little jammy doughnuts you always buy from Sainsbury's.'

'Well then I'll have to sniff each doughnut carefully before biting into them, like a dog detecting cancer.' He smiled. I was used to that smile now, but I grew fonder of it all the time.

I tapped the side of my nose. 'I'd buy the kind of poison that was undetectable. It would pass your little sniff test. And then I'd get rid of you in the foundations of the new halls they're building down the road.'

He kicked off his shoes and sat further back on my bed, stretching out his legs. His socks were made from thick blue wool and I had a strange urge to squeeze his toes affectionately. He asked me how I'd get his body over there in the first place.

It was a good point. 'Maybe I'd lure you over there – alive – and promise you a night of ravaging sex in the rubble.'

'And then you'd feed me a doughnut?'

I thought about it. 'You couldn't say no to a sweet treat. Or if I couldn't get your body all the way out there, I'd just hide it in the trees by the lake, as far as I could pull it in the night. I'd have to make sure you were hard to find in some way, even if I didn't have the strength to bury you. I could put you in some nice camouflage clothing. That'd buy me a day or two.'

He laughed. He set his mug down on the bedside cabinet and put his hand around my wrist. 'Would the poison hurt?'

'Maybe a bit, at first. You might vomit, before you die.'

He squeezed my wrist tighter so that my skin pinched.

'Ouch.'

He released it. 'Would you like to see me in a bit of pain?'

'Maybe I would. When Sofie was really pleased with your story and gushed over it, a part of me wanted to hurt you.'

He raised his eyebrows. He held out his wrist and told me to squeeze it. I clasped my hand around it lightly.

He looked at me. 'No, as hard as you can.'

I squeezed it harder and he laughed.

'Harder, Alice.'

My hand ached.

'I was happy when she liked my work.' He winced and breathed out. 'I felt like I'd won a little game.'

I released his wrist.

'You looked smug, then and now,' I told him.

We'd had a few classes by then where we'd read each other's work, but none of my pieces had been received as well as the secret story. In that class, Sofie called me out, used me as an example to the others of smooth time jumps and succinct writing. She had pointed at one of my last sentences, as the character left the pub and thought about her husband back home, and had even circled a word on the projector screen. 'These moments,' she said, 'are above rubies.' I wanted more of them.

'I only look smug now because you did what I told you to do,' he said.

I shrugged. 'You're convincing when you want to be.'

He put a hand on my thigh and started stroking it.

'Walt,' I said. 'That kiss was a mistake.'

He continued to stroke my leg. 'Why am I here then?'

I put my hand on his hand, feeling the grooves of his knuckles.

'I don't know if this is a good idea.' But the truth was, it felt as though it was the only good idea I'd had all year. I felt deceitful towards my boyfriend, but every day with Walt it seemed to matter less and less. I felt so comfortable with him that my other relationship started to feel superficial and awkward, and therefore less like I was doing anything wrong. When I was away from Walt, I would start to obsess over all the words he said to me. I tried to do the same with my boyfriend and struggled to remember any meaningful conversation we'd ever had.

'I like you so much,' Walt said. He looked at me properly for the first time.

It felt good to be touched and to be wanted. He tucked my hair behind my ear like he was taking care of me. I looked back at him. I wanted to ask him if he would kiss me now.

'I didn't know,' I said quietly, 'but I'm glad. I'm so glad.' I wasn't glad at all. I was terrified that he didn't mean it, and I wanted to kiss him so much. I thought he might get up and leave at any moment. But then, he did kiss me.

'I've been thinking about you non-stop since the party,' he told me when he drew back. I stood, pulled him up to the desk and unbuttoned my shirt. He put his hands on my stomach, then my breasts. I asked him if that was good and he said yes, his breath ragged. I felt insane in that moment, like I'd do anything if he asked me to. He pulled down my jeans and put his hand inside my underwear. He told me I felt so good. I thought I would come immediately just from the sound of his voice in my ear and the familiar smell of his body, so close to mine.

'Don't stop,' I said, and he pressed his whole body against mine. It felt like I could ask him to do anything and he would do it, too. I put my hands behind me on the desk and he pushed against me again. 'Okay,' I told him, and then, 'Please.'

He kissed my neck and I unbuttoned his jeans. He gasped when I touched him. 'I'm so happy,' I said.

I had imagined him touching me over and over again, so that the actual touching felt like a kind of drug. I told him he could do whatever he wanted, but he only pulled me onto the bed and lay on top of me, pushing into me deeper. He took a nipple in his mouth and I cried out.

When we were finished, I told him, 'I like *you* so much, too.' He was slumped over me, his stomach sticking to mine. He rolled onto his back, a hand on his forehead.

He shook his head, smiling. 'I've *always* liked you so much.'

I nuzzled into the crook of his shoulder as he put an arm around me.

'Say it again,' I said.

He kissed my head and said it again. I smoothed a hand over his chest, kissed his neck and bit his ear lobe gently. He leant his chin on top of my head and breathed out contentedly. 'Lucky me,' he said.

'That's the sex talking,' I said.

'No,' he said, 'that's the feeling I have when I'm with you.' He smiled and looked down at me. 'What are you thinking about?' He kissed my hand and waited.

I opened my mouth to tell him, when his phone buzzed. It was like an electric shock, both the sound of it in his jeans pocket on the floor, and his visible reaction to it. He sat upright as though he'd been exposed. His phone buzzed again. He looked down, pulling his arm from under me. His mind had left the room.

I shifted on the bed as he stood up. 'Someone's really blowing up your phone. Is everything all right?'

He turned round and smiled, but the smile didn't go anywhere. It was a reflex that never left his mouth. His eyes were solid blocks of dread and his neck looked so stiff, I thought I could snap it. 'Yeah, it's fine.' He started pulling on his clothes. 'It's just my mum. She's been calling a lot recently. I guess she's worried about me in a different country or something.'

He zipped up his jeans and walked over to the bookshelf, picking up my copy of *Tess of the D'Urbervilles*. It was the Roman Polanski film tie-in edition. 'Maybe she's right, you know. I think sometimes, she's right. That it was stupid to come all this way to write a book. I could do it anywhere. And why do I even want to do it so badly?'

I sat up and pulled my shirt back on, buttoning it up. 'Sofie said that if the idea of not writing a novel before you're forty makes you want to jump off a bridge, then you should be here.'

He put the book on my desk, still staring at the cover. 'Maybe if something so stupid makes you want to jump off a bridge, you should just jump.' He made a face that said: I'm joking. 'Sofie doesn't know shit.' He laughed mirthlessly. 'But she has all the codes.'

I frowned, my arms crossed over my knees on the bed.

'Don't forget that,' he continued. 'She's not even right most of the time, with her single-minded way of doing things. But that doesn't matter when you're the one in charge. She's the one that can make a difference for us. She's the one with access to the big red button.'

'You sound like a conspiracy theorist.'

His phone buzzed again. 'Sometimes I want to just throw it in the lake. It would be an easy kill.'

'Your mum would just email you instead.'

'That isn't the point.' He sat briefly on the desk chair to pull on his shoes, then went over to the door. 'She once said there must be something really interesting about words on a page if it stopped me from calling her. And I told her there was and she'd never understand it, but that wasn't why I didn't call.' He turned back and looked at me.

I didn't want him to leave, but I didn't know what to say.

'Because there is, isn't there? Something really interesting about words on a page? Writers are bound by their own secret worlds they go to all the time and can never explain. That's what makes it feel so good,' he said, 'because it does, it does, it does feel so good.'

He seemed angry at something, but I didn't know what. I nodded. 'It does,' I said.

Then he smiled, and his mind came back to the room. He knelt next to me on the bed.

'You look so good like that, all undone.' He kissed me on the forehead. 'I'll see you soon.' Then he left and his words went with him.

I lay back down on my bed and called my boyfriend. 'If you were going to kill me, how would you do it?'

He asked me what the hell I was going on about.

Six

Robert told us that our worst nightmares were great material for our novels. It was one of many aphorisms he doled out in each of his classes, presumably compiled from pithy observations made by other writers, as well as from his own experience. Some were genuinely helpful (ask a big question at the beginning of the novel and then delay it until the end), while others were less so, given we were being workshopped every week (write without fear of being read).

He told us to be unkind to our characters and wait to see how they'd react.

'Books are made up of choices,' he said, fingering the lapel of his tweed jacket. It was autumn, the cold afternoon air hitting the single glazing of our seminar room. I looked out at the campus beyond our little room with the purple chairs and felt important that I was inside, talking about books.

'The more choices the better. When someone's pushed into a corner, the choices they make reveal something about themselves and that moves the plot forwards.'

We nodded and took notes.

'The choices could look like a family tree, one decision branching out after another. It is a useful exercise to just sit and write as many choices as possible for your characters in any given situation. What would they do next? The choices create consequences, and every great novel has consequences. The consequences can then create a sense of doom that the character has to work their way out of. Even books where it appears nothing is happening are often tightly plotted in this way.'

He turned towards Grace.

'Grace's latest piece was a great example of this. You have hopefully all read the scene she submitted this week. It's contained and sparse: two lovers wake up in bed together, sticky sheets entangle their limbs. But something isn't quite right, and unsettling memories are revealed from the night before.'

He invited us all to pull out her piece and mark up every moment where the main character makes a choice. We took out our pens and underlined certain passages: when the character decides to leave the room and lock herself in the bathroom. The decisions she made the night before: accepting his invitation to drink more wine, stay longer, kiss him.

Grace looked down at her notebook and half-heartedly took down our suggestions for how to create more intrigue and drama.

'It would've been better if you'd made this moment longer,' Henderson said.

Walt told her that something about the tense felt wrong and it would seem more uncanny if she switched perspectives without giving too much away. Beatrice said the entire thing seemed faultless, apart from when the character gets back into bed with him. Why would she do that?

'Aha,' Robert said. 'A big choice. One that reveals something important.' Grace looked up at him as though she was at the dentist and was waiting for him to take his fingers out of her mouth. 'But what about the micro choices, too? The ones that are subtle, almost imperceptible?' He lifted the piece out in front of him and paced the room, like he was in a play. He started reading it out loud and

Grace shut her notebook so it made a little slap. *'When it was over,'* he read, *'he went to the bathroom and returned with a roll of toilet paper, which he dropped next to me, not waiting for me to reach out and accept it. I lay there, waiting for him to say something, but instead he sat and watched me. I wondered if he expected me to run a delighted hand over what he'd deposited on me, but instead I wiped it away methodically, ripping off piece after piece of tissue as though I was cleaning a greasy work surface.'*

Robert took a step towards Grace's desk. He looked like he was giving her a sermon. He enunciated every word like we might miss something important. Grace's hair fell untucked from her ear as she lowered her head. The whole thing felt oddly humiliating. I glanced at Walt who was looking up at Robert, frowning. Robert smiled almost gleefully in Grace's direction as he read the last two sentences. *'I wiped until the paper became damp, my skin prickling in response. I dropped the encrusted tissue at his feet and then, as an afterthought, licked my fingers while he looked at me.'* Robert drew out the word 'licked', his tongue protruding with exaggerated effect from his mouth.

'It's just perfect,' he said, and Grace lifted her head up. 'Her sexual partner has dropped a roll of toilet paper next to her. She is passive, vulnerable.' He stroked his jacket again in thought. 'But she has one little choice left while his attention is on her: what should she do with it?' He told Grace she was clever, and I smiled. It was, after all, nice to be told this. Sometimes it felt like the whole point of coming to class.

Grace shifted in her seat and clicked a lid onto her biro. She didn't smile or appear bashful. She didn't seem to react in any way. Robert continued on about balancing characters' needs and their wants. I felt envious of how brilliant her story was and wondered why she hadn't said thank you when it was recognised.

Robert invited us to comment further on the piece and I heaped more praise on her. She became more animated when the other students spoke and opened her notebook back up.

'I read the whole thing in an excited rush,' I told her. She looked like she didn't know what to say. 'It was oddly relatable,' I added, imagining this was the kind of thing I'd like to hear, even if it was only half true. She smiled at me, her pen hovering above the page, but didn't write anything down.

We moved on to workshopping Beatrice's piece and I watched Robert's face while the students talked. His eyes flicked back towards Grace, just for a moment, but she was lost in thought, tapping her biro on the table. He ran a hand back and through his hair as he turned away. It was a small, unconscious movement, but I could tell he was still thinking about her story.

I wanted the class to be over. Sometimes the very act of analysing it started to make the writing feel bad. I wanted Grace to be left alone with her story, even if the whole intention had been to share it.

When everyone filed out to go to the pub afterwards, I hovered next to Grace as she packed up her bag. Robert came over and recommended a novel he'd just read that he thought we might like. We both smiled and I made a show of writing it down. He congratulated Grace again on her piece and she said she'd written the whole thing at the last minute. 'It could've been better, maybe, but it was okay.' She zipped up her rucksack and then moved towards the door. As we passed, Robert curled a hand around her jacket shoulder. I looked at its meaty weight pressed against the soft washed denim of her arm. 'Good work,' he said.

We set off towards the pub in silence, trying to catch up with the others. I was thinking about how I could be more like her. I was envious of how the words seemed to come out of her, simple and succinct and fully formed, even in 500-word chunks. I wanted to ask her if she still wrote poetry and what her favourite novel was. I wanted to ask her if she'd thought about the plot for her dissertation and what she would write. Everything seemed so optimistic for her, like her talent had a momentum all of its own, whether she liked it or not.

'I can't tell whether he just has a writerly interest in you, or whether it's something else,' I said instead.

'He's just a bit of a creep, that's all,' she said. 'But it's harmless.'

'You wrote something vulnerable, but clever, like he said.'

She grimaced, pulling her rucksack strap further up her shoulder. She shrugged. 'I just write down what's in my head. He's the one that makes it weird. Don't we all have thoughts about things like that? We just don't ever talk about it.'

I agreed with her and we kept walking. 'I guess all he did was read it out loud. But sometimes that's enough. To be read out loud and to see the look on someone's face when they do it.'

She laughed. She agreed the look on his face was vile. 'I sometimes feel like Sofie and Robert are the ones that get in the way of good writing, not us. Do you ever think that? That it might be easier if we actually just wrote on our own, without every sentence being analysed in front of the whole class?'

I considered it. 'No,' I said, 'not really.'

At the pub, she ordered three packets of crisps and splayed them open for the table. We drank pints and gingerly lifted the salty snacks into our mouths, while Grace spoke very little and devoured crisp after crisp. When she finished one packet, she licked a finger and dragged it across the reflective sheen of the salty plastic. Walt mentioned how enamoured Robert had been with her today and she trailed her finger along the packet corner in search of more crumbs.

'If I'm being honest, I thought it might be expected of me at some point to sleep with him,' she said. 'So the fact it isn't like that is a relief.'

Walt shook his head, staring down at the empty wrapper. 'Robert?' He snorted to himself. 'He wouldn't have the guts. He wouldn't even know what to do with you.' I bridled at the implication that Walt *would* know.

Grace sucked the last of the salt from her index finger in distracted thought. 'You're right,' she said, as though this had just occurred to her for the very first time. 'He's not one of the ones to worry about.' After a moment's pause, they looked at each other and laughed.

Later that week, Walt asked me to go on a walk with him around the greenery by the Brutalist buildings that housed our living quarters. We decided that fresh air might help us with ideas for our latest pieces, but we ended up talking about past relationships instead.

'I always have break-ups on trains,' he said. 'Maybe it's subconscious, like I don't want them to make a scene.'

'It's why people have deep conversations in cars,' I said. 'It's easier to talk when you're not looking at each other.'

'Even though on a train you can sit opposite each other, watching an expression of horror unfold on their face.'

We walked towards the large pond at the end of the grounds. It was encircled by trees, but during the summer, people were known to slip down its silty banks and go for a dip. I imagined my face under the water, the relief of being submerged. It wasn't quite cold enough for a big coat yet, and I knew the water would be around 18 degrees.

'You always have an answer for everything, don't you, Alice?'

'It's just a theory.'

'When we break up, where should we do it?'

I hit him on the arm. 'I thought we were meant to be talking about writing. Not our theoretical relationship.'

He nodded. 'It's too bad. I would've been a good boyfriend. Not to the others, of course, but to you. I would never break up with you on a train.'

'But you'd still break up with me.'

He smiled. 'We can talk about writing if you want,' he said. 'Tell me about your latest piece. Or wait for the workshop to rip it to shreds as a little treat.'

I stared at the dark water, the reeds surrounding it. A group of ducks sailed past. 'I like being read in a group, you know. It's validating.'

'Have we been going to the same classes?'

'Before coming here, the only person who ever read a thing I wrote was my boyfriend,' I said. 'And he would labour through every sentence and entirely – deliberately – miss the point of everything.' I realised I was absent-mindedly taking off my jumper, unbuttoning my top shirt button.

'Still soldiering on with the literary hero then?'

'I suppose I haven't found the words yet,' I said. 'But I will.'

'It's okay.' He didn't look at me. 'I get it.'

'I don't think I ever wanted that much from him when he read my work. It would've been nice for him to say he really felt something about that character. That he empathised with a thought or a feeling. It would be nice for him to be moved, or laugh.'

'You mean it would be nice for him to express an emotion.'

I thought about this. 'That's not so easy for men. They're taught their whole lives to do the opposite.' I slipped off my shoes.

Walt looked down at me and did the same. 'I tell you things, but you don't seem to always want to hear them. You're always asking for people's emotions, but if I tell you something, you brush over it.'

I shook my head. 'Don't do that. We're going swimming. Can't we just go swimming?'

'I want to tell you about my mother and my childhood and my whole life, but sometimes I think you just want the version of me that's written down. You only care when it's part of a story.'

'I care, Walt. Of course I care.' I wanted to tell him that he was wrong. It was easier to love him on the page because the page couldn't let me down. 'I'm going to end it,' I said.

The sun was low in the sky. There were three or four hours of daylight left but only one with the light peeking through the trees. Everyone was inside, working. I took off my shirt and laid it on the side of the pond. I rolled off my jeans and stood in my underwear, not looking at him. 'I just didn't know what you wanted. I *don't* know what you want.' It was all his fault. I didn't ask to feel this way about him. It just happened to me, like the weather. I just had to wait for it to pass. 'I like reading the sad things you write.' I pressed a toe into the silty mud and he harrumphed at me. 'I'm serious. People don't laugh things off in their writing. They feel pain.'

'I feel pain.'

'I know.' I crossed my arms across my bare stomach. 'I wasn't sure at first. I wasn't sure you weren't entirely spoilt.'

'That's a double negative.'

'We're not workshopping. We're swimming.'

'I'm not spoilt. I just lived in a different country.'

'You had a housemaid.'

He started unbuckling his trousers. He slipped off his T-shirt. My arms started to goosebump. I thought the moment had gone. The light had changed. It felt strange to be standing there like that.

'You have plenty of people to talk to on the course besides me,' I said sulkily. 'What about Henderson? What about Grace? There's something charming about the way she writes. There's something charming about the way she does *everything*.'

He dismissed my comment with a wave of his hand. 'What do you want a boyfriend like that to read your work for anyway? Why don't you leave the reading to the people who care – the writers?'

'He's not all bad, you know.'

'Well, no one's all bad, Alice. Not even you.' He smiled at me, but I looked down at my feet. The bank of the pond was starting to stick between my toes. 'I'm not sure I can get in now. I might change my mind.' I looked over and he was naked. His body was soft like an animal and I wanted to touch it.

He smiled at me, unabashed. Then he took some cautious steps towards the water and slipped right in. He let out a gasp and sailed forward, splashing his arms in front crawl. After a minute, he turned round and floated on his back.

'How's the water?' I shouted to him.

He laughed. 'Wet.'

I looked down at my clothes.

He asked if I wanted to get in. I said no, not any more. He told me I'd feel good afterwards. That if I got in, I'd feel good and that we could go back to his dorm or my dorm and feel good together.

'I don't want to.'

'I know you do,' he shouted up to the sky. 'You haven't lived yet, you haven't lived. You don't know what you take for granted. The water feels good,' he shouted at the top of his lungs.

'You've read too much David Foster Wallace.'

'Well, one of us has to.' He swum towards me.

'I watched his commencement address on YouTube.'

He came towards the edge of the bank to a point where he could stand in the water. 'Were you moved by it?'

'Yes,' I said, 'very much. But I am also moved by other, smaller things. And you're right. I do want to be with you, just for the company. Just to lie in bed and listen to Spotify together afterwards and talk about the books on each other's shelves. I just want to be with you for the intimacy.'

'Yes, all of that,' he said. 'But I also just want to be with you so I can touch you.'

I nodded. 'I'm not swimming.'

He got out, dripping. 'Don't make me say something completely banal, Alice. Don't make me tell you to leave him. I'm about to freeze my bollocks off. We'd best be getting on back home.'

Posted by ManofConsonantSorrow

Any other men been sexually harassed? What's your story?
1,345 comments

NumberOneBen_83
I remember at school, there was a rumour going round about the size of my junk. At first it was kind of flattering, but it got old really quickly. To settle a bet, one of the girls grabbed my crotch and everyone laughed. She said it was fine because she didn't want to do anything with it, it was just for fun. Still creeps me out to this day.

Kermit_The_Pog
I used to work at a bar, so I have *a lot* of stories. But one evening I was bartending at a private gig and the couple whose house it was came into the kitchen and tried to take my shirt off. The woman was grabbing me and the man started unbuckling my belt. I fought them off (I was much bigger than both of them) and then I got out of there as quick as I could. I didn't get paid, but they also ended up without a bartender for their party.

Toastertime21
When I was a child, my aunt used to stay with us at Christmas. One night I woke up in my bed and she was looming over me, her hand down my pyjama trousers. She said she was just 'tucking me in', but there was something really weird about it. I tried to tell my parents, but they just laughed and said I secretly wanted a goodnight kiss from Auntie. Now that I think about it, it was really fucked up.

PembertonRoad267
There's a woman I work with who's married with two kids, but

has definitely always had a crush on me. At every opportunity she jokes about how we're going to go out on a date and how she can't wait to get divorced so she can marry me instead. She works in HR so won't approve my annual leave until I come over to her desk and talk to her. She always jokes that she's going to take the same week off so we can run away together. I feel like I can't say anything as she just thinks it's a hilarious long-standing joke. She's the only one laughing.

Seven

Before the end of the first term, it was my turn to be workshopped again and I needed a story. Our latest assignment was on unreliable narrators. We were free to write a story with a narrator as mad, bad or dangerous as we wanted – or we could explore the extent to which *every* first-person narrator is delusional. Sofie was keen to emphasise this last point, that we are the ultimate unreliable narrator. We rationalise everything that happens to us, turning it into a story and making ourselves the hero.

'It's an actual psychological phenomenon in the brains of healthy people,' she said. 'We imagine that our lives are about continuous improvement. We set new goals and we strive to meet them. We imagine that things will get better. When people say in response to your work – because they will – that we don't need fiction, I would say: we are fiction. We tell ourselves stories in order to make sense of everything we see and feel and experience. The best story we'll ever tell is ourselves. This is okay, because it's the only way to be. Imagine a world where our mass of experiences had no sense of order at all. Imagine only thinking things would get worse. Life would barely be worth living. But, putting aside the fact that your greatest piece of work is your own life, there is real work to be done. Keep writing,' she said.

I took my notebook to the juice kitchen and hoped that after my shift I might have time to write down some thoughts in the back office. I stood next to Olena and labelled each bottle for the day's orders. Earlier that day, they'd run out of spinach, so Olena had texted me to bring some from Tesco's. When I arrived, she took the bags without looking at me, and said I should keep quiet about this as they weren't organic. 'But we need it to finish the mixing.'

She always seemed more upset than I was at the idea of pouring chemical-laden spinach juice into a £14 bottle of goodness to unsuspecting customers. What would they know if it was organic or not? But, despite her secret mobile phone, Olena was good. Even though Molly was never anywhere to be found, Olena always wanted to do the right thing.

After I'd packed every bottle of juice into its cool bag, Olena cracked open a three-day-old litre bottle of cucumber. I had other tasks I was meant to be getting on with, negotiating the price of cashews and researching new recipes, but I was tired and wanted to sit with Olena instead.

'It will just go to waste,' she said, offering me a glass. While I waited for the courier, she sat with me in the office. She asked me about my writing and sipped on her juice, making a face. I told her about the week's assignment.

'Do you like writing about bad people?'

'Well, sometimes. But they don't have to be bad, just flawed. Like, we're not always the best storytellers of our own lives. We forget things. Or we misremember. We fill in gaps. Or we lie to ourselves, deliberately. Actually, maybe that is bad.'

Olena nodded. 'Sometimes it's easier to make sense of things that have no sense.' She took out her old phone and laid it next to her smartphone on the table. She pointed to them. 'No sense,' she said. I laughed. 'But imagine what lies you must tell yourself to pay for this stuff every day,' she raised her glass. The cucumber juice she could just about manage, but the other greens made her want to vomit. What was so bad about *eating* your vegetables anyway?

Molly had recently given Olena a three-day juice cleanse as a gift.

'I drank the ones I liked, the little lemon shots. The rest, I poured down the sink. But Molly still complimented me afterwards, saying my skin was glowing and I had lost weight. Molly thought I'd done it, and it didn't make a difference if I had or not. Maybe I'm the liar, but she also sees what she wants to. I told her what she wanted to hear, which was that it was awful, I'd felt sick, had the shakes and constipation. Then,' she said, 'I told her at the end I felt great. But really I felt great because I'd just eaten the same old stuff, cookies and jam. And she was happy because she thought she'd done something good for me.' She shrugged. 'But I don't need the juice, I just need the job.'

'How are things going at home?' I asked.

'I don't know what to do or how things will end.' She nibbled at her fingernails. 'Do you think you will marry your boyfriend?'

My first reaction was to laugh, but then I stopped myself. It shouldn't have been such an absurd question because I was supposed to love him. I'd chosen him, even if we'd just met through friends at university. I had initially liked him because when I met him, he was sitting on the floor of his bedroom in the flat he shared with my friend and was wearing a nice shirt. He seemed a normal kind of person that did a normal kind of job.

She looked at me shrewdly. 'If you don't want to marry him, Alice, you shouldn't be with him. Trust me, I know.'

'I'm still in my twenties, I don't know if I even want to get married.'

She smiled at me. 'You will. You wait and see.'

'I admit that you were right about your first point, maybe it is better to not be with him at all. What do you think it is about your friend that you're drawn to? More than your husband?'

She frowned and clicked a button on both phones as though checking there was no one listening at the other end.

'He talks to me. I feel lonely all the time. I have work and I have him. At least you have writing.'

'Does it feel like your friend is something of your own?' I asked her.

She smiled. 'Yes, it is nice to have a secret even if it is bad. It is nice to tell someone how I feel every day and he tells me how he feels, too. He tells me about all the different houses he goes into and how other people live. The strange things they have there and the things they tell him, because people tell their electricians everything. Then he fixes things for them and leaves, and they forget all about him.'

She said his name was Alan. I asked her if she felt comfortable with him after what had happened between them.

'It made me realise I want to be with him. But I can't, so I just told him that we could still be together but not *together*, you know.' She looked down at her juice. 'Does that sound like a bad deal for him?'

'I don't know. It can be nice to be around people that bring you joy, even if you can't have all of it.'

'I have now started going to his house and telling my husband I go spinning. I don't let him touch me, not after last time. But I let him ask me. Sometimes I let him ask until he's laughing so much he's crying,' she smiled, looking down at her two phones. 'Last time, I got undressed and lay on his bed. He was so good, because he didn't try anything. He just watched me.'

'And did you enjoy the watching, too?' I asked her.

'Yes, very much. Does it sound awful? I like to feel free, and when I'm there I feel totally free. Sometimes I even forget he's next to me, sometimes I fall asleep. Other times I let him lie next to me.' She put her cucumber juice down to put her head in her hands. 'You must think I'm crazy.'

'I really don't. I can imagine a world where you couldn't be with someone but yearned to be, so much so that it became worth being with them in a less than ideal way. But, maybe by simply being there and feeling like this, and exposing yourself to him, you've already broken all those rules?' I said gently. 'If your marriage is romantically over anyway, would it be such a stretch to leave him for Alan?'

'The rules have not been broken,' she insisted, her cheeks flaming red. 'I have remained faithful, I have done what I promised God I would do on my wedding day. I haven't been with another man even if I did lie next to him. Even if sometimes, I let him touch himself next to me, and I touched myself too, we never touched each other. This is an important difference in the eyes of God.'

I looked at her sceptically, but didn't want to sound dismissive.

'How do you know God has such fine lines? And where they start or end?'

She drank the rest of her juice and sighed.

'Why do you feel it's okay to hate someone, to wish someone dead even, but never actually harm them? You just know. There's a line. It's God's line.'

It was true, I thought, this kind of line existed around us and everything we did all the time. Even if we didn't believe in God, we felt bound by some social contract to behave in the right way. The line was often crossed and we had a feeling while we were doing it. But sometimes by crossing it, the line would move and the feeling would go away.

'Maybe it would be better to just be honest and tell your husband,' I said. 'Because now you think you're doing the right thing, but sooner or later you'll cross that line of yours. Maybe it would be better to do the thing you think is bad, like leaving your husband, in order to make being with Alan good.' I didn't want her to hate herself for the situation she'd ended up in. Her face was troubled. I could imagine her sitting at home and working out the imaginary contracts with God that surrounded her marriage. I could imagine her drawing out in her mind what was right and wrong and sticking to it doggedly.

She smiled.

'You are so English. You are like this because you come from an island nation. It makes you think that the individual is all that matters, that your own needs are more important than anything else. English people think they're special and unique, but you only think that because of your geography. You only think it because of the . . .' she gestured in the air '. . . the green hills and the grey rivers and the sea that separates you from everyone else.'

I laughed.

'There might be some truth in that, but I can't help but want to be happy.' I put a hand on her arm. 'I want you to be happy, too. That's the most important thing, isn't it? God would want you to be happy, wouldn't he?'

She thought about this.

'No,' she said, 'not at all.'

The piece I wrote for class came onto the page easily. It was about two people who were caught up in an affair. They spent afternoons in the park together and shared intimacies, and even sexual encounters, but because they never touched each other, the narrator was determined that they hadn't done anything morally wrong. The character was deluded but also left out key pieces of information, leading the reader to believe by the end that they'd had a full-blown physical affair anyway.

The class agreed it was an interesting conundrum.

Walt said, 'But touching each other is the biggest part of any affair, so you're alluding to a deal that is always on the cusp of being broken. The laws of probability say it will be. If it isn't, it's still an affair, not just because of the non-physical ways you can cheat on a partner, but because the very notion of their deal means they will break it.'

He looked right at me as he said, 'That's where the sexual tension lies, in the not touching, and that's why it would soon become completely irresistible. They would have been better off never acknowledging it in the first place. The acknowledgement to not do something was when the affair started.'

I watched his face as he spoke, as though he was talking about a piece of work that had nothing to do with me. I realised he had created his own lines and rules in his head, boundaries he might have set out for the two of us that I had no say in.

'But,' he said with emphasis, 'I did like the piece, so much. We're all sitting here arguing about it aren't we, so it must be powerful?'

In truth, I didn't care too much about any of this. I was waiting until Sofie would pull my piece up on the screen. I wanted her to tell me it was well written. The content of what I'd actually written didn't matter that much, I just wanted to be told it was good. The anticipation was awful. But as Sofie scrolled through the piece and at the end congratulated me with the line, 'It's the whole trick!' I felt elated.

Walt smiled and nodded, impressed. Then after the class, he asked me if I'd ever let him touch me again.

We were walking past the Students' Union.

'I know part of the fun is the sort of "will they, won't they",' he said, 'but I'm leaning towards they will.'

'The story wasn't about you, Whitman.'

'It was a little bit.' He lowered his voice as Stella and Beatrice shouted goodbye at us from across the way, headed towards the car park. 'And I get it. It's interesting that all your stories are about some sort of sexual conundrum.'

I laughed sarcastically. 'They're just about people doing what people do.'

'No different from Austen then.'

I took that seriously. 'Not really, if you think Austen was just critiquing social customs.'

'And our social customs are about jacking off in front of each other?'

'Could we stop talking about this?'

'I can tell I'm annoying you.'

'Sometimes you do annoy me, yes. Mainly when you're speaking.'

'I just thought someone should say, even if Sofie won't, that while your stories are engrossing in a writing seminar, I'd be careful when you come to plotting your novel. Who's going to read 80,000 words about unfulfilled sexual urges?'

'Isn't there an entire industry of teen fiction dedicated to that?'

The path opened up to the wide green space that led to the lake.

'If we're together,' he said, 'the urges won't be unfulfilled. You'll be free to write about something else.'

'It really wasn't about us.'

He laughed and pulled on his rucksack straps. 'So I'm not always on your mind then? How disappointing.'

I stopped walking and turned to look at his face. The same face he always had, the same one he would always have. 'What are we doing?'

His hair was soft in the breeze and his eyebrows moved together in confusion. I wanted to smooth a hand over his cheek and feel the texture of it.

'That's what I'm asking you, Alice. Named after the book, I presume?'

'Yes, but *A Town Like*, not *in Wonderland*.'

'I can make it easier for you.' He smiled, 'I can tell you what to do.'

I told myself I would never be with a writer. Writers were bad for each other, like fleas trying to feed on the same piece of skin. But I thought of Olena and how she was right. He talked to me.

I told him I'd see him later, then I walked back to my room and called my boyfriend. I told him it had to be over, even though I felt I still loved him. I told him there wasn't anyone else, but I just couldn't do this any more.

'Just like that?'

'I know it feels just like that to you, but it's actually been a very long time.'

He sighed.

'Do you realise there is something very deeply wrong with you? Do you know that as long as you act like this you'll never be happy?'

'I don't think you can decide that,' I said.

'It isn't about deciding. But it's true, it just is. I suppose you'll be wanting your stuff back.'

'Maybe at some point, I don't know.'

'I'll keep it all because you'll probably change your mind.'

I told him he could give my clothes away but I wanted my books. 'It isn't about happiness anyway, it really isn't.'

He grunted and hung up the phone.

Later that day, I had a session with Sofie in her office to discuss my piece. I got there early and sat on a chair outside her door. She appeared a few minutes later holding a coffee and she smiled and gestured for me to come inside. She shared an office with a few of the other tutors, but none of them were around. She put a university branded mug down by her laptop and I sat on the armchair opposite her desk, leaning forward. As she took off her jacket, a beautifully textured boucle wool that I wanted very badly to stroke, I noted aloud that she didn't have her usual standout mug with her.

She let out a little 'huh' and rolled her eyes. 'It's kitsch but I love that thing. I can't find it. I must have left it somewhere.'

I thought about being the kind of favourite student who gets her a mug with nipples on that she still uses exclusively years later. I thought maybe I could buy her a replacement when I left the course, something with a little in-joke between the two of us. I watched her prise my printed sheets of writing from her perfectly aged leather satchel, flicking through them with a long, wine-coloured fingernail.

'Before we start, are you okay? You look like you've been crying.'

I shook my head. 'Someone said something bad about me earlier and I guess I kind of took it to heart.'

'We're writers, that's what we do. That's why the whole thing works.'

'Sometimes I want a day off from it. Robert says when you're a writer you don't get days off, anyway. Even when you're not writing you're thinking about it.'

She nodded at me, as though she was listening intently. 'Robert subscribes to the method acting school of writing. I don't know. I think sometimes, you're allowed to think of yourself as just a human first.' She smiled. The undivided attention made me feel nervous and I stumbled over my words, looking above her desk at the newspaper clippings she'd carefully placed there. I pointed to a Graham Greene quote and told her it was one of my favourites.

She tapped the paper in front of her.

'Your recent piece was excellent. I love this character you've used a couple of times. She is raw, vulnerable. She feels very real.'

I nodded and wondered whether I should be taking notes.

'Have you thought about using her as a character in your novel? The plotting seminars are fast approaching and I think there's something here.'

'I'm not sure it could sustain a whole book,' I said.

'Well, you'd have to figure that out. But I think there's good material here.' She took out some designer tortoiseshell glasses and peered down at the words. 'Your writing is very pared back, it's tight.' She put her hand into a fist and I wondered if she realised she was doing it. 'On a sentence level, it's very exciting.'

I didn't want to ask what she thought of it on a page level. I nodded, not knowing what to do with my hands, feeling my cheeks light up like a furnace.

'And I would help you.' She took off her glasses and looked straight at me. 'I really want to help you with your work.'

I couldn't help but grin at this, and she offered me a small smile back. She opened her hands out. 'I know people, you know. My recommendations carry a lot of weight.'

I didn't say I already knew this. I felt my knee shaking and put a hand on it to stop it.

'That would be amazing.' I swallowed. 'Thank you so much.'

She nodded as though it was settled. 'You might have to work a bit on the plot,' she said, waving her glasses in one hand. 'But I think if you keep exploring what's driving her, what choices she'll make to try and solve these inner conflicts, there's really something there. You have to keep mining the character.' She tapped the side of her head. 'Keep going deeper. It can be hard to pull off this kind of confessional fiction, but I think the only way to do it is to look it in the eye. Gut everything from your life and don't worry about burning bridges.'

I looked at her, realising that what she'd meant by her gesture was that I already had been mining my own life. Not just things I absorbed or stories I heard. She thought the character was me. As she ran through my piece, giving her feedback line by line, I didn't correct her. It was well known that she loved auto-fiction because that's what she wrote, and it was true I wanted to be like her. But what I realised as I sat there, looking attentively into her beautiful face, was that she really thought I *was* like her, and that's why she wanted to help me.

At the end of our session, she said she hoped she'd given me enough to think about.

'Hold your head up high,' she said, 'and don't worry if people say nasty things to you. I often find that what people say about you is a bigger reflection on them.'

I put my bag on my shoulder and agreed. It meant nothing.

Walking home, I felt better than I had in months. I wanted to call my parents to tell them that I'd had a good day, like a child released from school. I approached the grey building I lived in, the staggered levels and jutting balconies on the upper floors, and I felt that everything ugly could be beautiful.

The next thing I did was walk to Walt's building and knock on his door. I wanted to tell him that I didn't have a boyfriend any more, but he was distracted. He let me in and asked what was going on. When I said nothing, smiling, he sat back at his desk and hunched over his laptop.

'This bloody thing isn't quite working today and I can't work out why,' he said.

'Can you just, can you look at me for a second?'

He continued to frown at the screen. 'I might switch it all to third person. I think it'll help. *He* thinks it'll help.'

'Walt.' I went and put a hand on his shoulder, a gesture that I felt was generous considering he was ignoring me. It startled him and he looked up at me.

'Sorry,' he said. 'Probably time to take a break anyway. Was there something you wanted to talk about?'

His expression was concerned and sweet. I liked watching him struggle with his work. It made me feel less insane about the hours I spent annoyed at my laptop, not producing anything.

'I think about you all the time,' I started. He opened his mouth to interrupt but I got there first. 'Well, you know, recently. I've thought about you recently. All the time at university and in the jobs I had afterwards, I only wanted to be somewhere else and with different people. This is the first time I've felt like I'm in the right place. And not just because I'm doing something I like, but I feel like I've found my people. Never in my whole life have I had people I could talk to about writing.' I gestured around me.

He remained sitting in his chair, looking up at me expectantly. His laptop screen went dark. He nodded. 'That's great.'

'We're all so different,' I said, 'but we have this one very important thing in common. And sometimes it makes me feel jealous that I'm actually not that special and sometimes it makes me want to scream with joy because finally it all makes sense. Finally, I'm not crazy.' I realised I hadn't taken off my coat or put my bag down. I slipped them off and then sat on his bed, and he came and sat beside me. He told me I sounded happy.

'I am, but I also feel awful.' My hands were in my lap and I stared at them, unable to look into his face. A face that had gone from nothing to everything in a matter of weeks. Now I wanted his face around me to look at all the time.

'I really like you,' I said. 'It doesn't matter that I had a boyfriend and that Stella and Beatrice make jokes about the way you write women. I just like you and I feel better when I'm with you.'

'Look at you, just look at you.' He was stroking my hair.

He put his fingers on my neck and without looking up I told him that I wanted him to touch me again. I wanted him to touch me over and over again. 'Because you're right. This whole thing is nothing without the touching part.'

He laughed and leaned towards me, burying his face in my neck.

'You smell so good. That's when I knew I really liked you, because on a chemical level you just smell so good.' He kissed my ear and I breathed out quietly. 'Had a boyfriend? You said, you *had* a boyfriend.'

'It's over, it should've been over a while ago.' I turned my face up to his, and he kissed me. I leaned closer and he put his hands around my back.

After a moment he pulled away and exhaled, still holding me. 'I needed that after today,' he said. 'And I'm glad you don't listen to what the Bitches of Eastwick say about my writing.'

'The what?'

'Stella and Beatrice. You know, like the Witches—'

I interrupted him. 'No, I get it. I just . . . that's so strange.'

He nipped at my bottom lip. 'Let's not talk,' he said. 'I finally have your attention.'

'You always had my attention.'

'I should hope so. I swam in a lake for you.' His lips grazed my nose. 'I got naked for you. Now it's your turn.'

I smiled as he fumbled at my chunky knitted jumper. He took off his T-shirt and lay beside me on the bed, moving his hand down my back and drawing circles on my waist. He pushed me down gently, then moved his hand up my stomach and kissed my belly button. I closed my eyes and let out a laugh. When I opened them again, he was looking up and smiling at me.

'You were right about the smell on a chemical level,' I told him. 'It's strong, it's good.'

'Oh, Alice.' He reached for the button on my jeans.

I felt his hot mouth on my neck, his fingers slick inside me. I told him how much I wanted him. I moved on top of him, his neck arching backwards. I put a hand on his chest and asked him if it was good and he grabbed me, pulling me closer to him. I leant forward, my hair falling over him. He touched me and told me he wanted to make me come.

I loved hearing him talk like this, and repeated the words in my head as I felt the warm glow inside me build and build.

'That's good,' I said, 'that's so good.' He groaned when I spoke, *hmm*, his face intensely serious. He pushed me onto my back and kissed me.

'I could do this forever,' he said.

Afterwards, I wiped a finger over my lip and sighed contentedly.

I looked towards his bedside table. I don't know what distracted me, but my brain kept telling me there was something there I had to look at. I could feel his mouth nudging my cheek, warm and soft, but all I could do was stare at what was there, next to his lamp.

I listened to the sound of my heart; if we can ever hear such a thing, that's when I heard it. I just stared. I knew soon that he would lift his head and he'd see what I was seeing. I knew soon that the illusion would be ruined, but I couldn't look away.

'Alice, what's wrong?'

I couldn't say. I raised a finger and just pointed at it.

He propped himself up on his elbows and looked towards where I was pointing, at the ceramic mug, the pink and purple nipples, the speckled paint rising like a spattered bruise. He inhaled sharply. 'Oh that, it's . . .' His face was pink, but it flushed an extra shade darker.

He looked at me. 'It's nothing,' he said weakly, in a way that told me it was really something.

I waited for an explanation. I waited for anything.

'It's hers,' I said, pointing at it again. I didn't want to say her name. I felt embarrassed.

He pulled on his T-shirt and stood beside the bed. 'I know what you're thinking, but it's not exactly what you're thinking.'

I pulled my top down over my stomach and asked him if she'd been here.

He nodded, reaching his arms out. 'Yes, but—'

'Why?'

Here, he paused. He tried to grab for me, but I was already pulling my jumper back on. 'What the fuck,' I said.

He grabbed at me again, scratching my arm. I would've told him not to touch me, but I couldn't bring myself to say it. I stopped and stared at him. He let go of me.

'Alice, I care about you so much. So much.'

I cared about him too. But I didn't say so.

I grabbed my coat and bag and opened the door without looking at him. I hesitated before letting the door close behind me, but I couldn't think of a thing to say. In the hallway, it was quiet. I could hear the whir from the electric lights. The carpet was still grey and the walls were still yellow.

It reminded me that everything changes just as quickly as nothing does.

Rebecca Sarah Ley

From: S.Muller1@gmail.com
To: Waltwonders89@gmail.com
Date: 5 December 2018, 18:11

Hi Walt,

I know last time we workshopped your piece we were talking about unreliable narrators. We also talked about obsession over a crime and how your narrator might react. I saw *The Conversation* at the BFI over the weekend, have you seen it?

It might spark inspiration, particularly around surveillance (watching and being watched). Anyway, it's a great film: a quiet, classic thriller with an abundance of intrigue.

Watch it. And keep writing.

So long and warmly,

Sofie

Eight

There was an air of collective unhappiness the next time we met as a group. Grace had written us all an email after the last workshop, trying to gauge our feelings on Sofie Muller's teaching methods. Several students immediately hit back, saying if we couldn't hack this kind of schedule and feedback, we'd never make it as writers.

Beatrice agreed. We need thick skins, she wrote. Writing 2,000 words a week is nothing really, when you've got to write a novel. Sofie knows what she's doing, whether you like her books or not.

That claim was undisputed.

I felt the worst for Henderson, who had become like a dog with his nose tapped. He admitted to feeling depressed about his writing in a way he couldn't shake. Yes, Sofie had been harsh to him, he wrote, but he didn't want that to affect anyone else's view of the course. He had to figure it out on his own, that's all.

We were nearing the end of the first term and decided to meet for coffee in the university building before our workshop. I was there early, sitting at a table stirring a frothy cappuccino. I hadn't told anyone what I'd seen in Walt's room and wouldn't even know how to voice it. I hadn't seen or heard from him for days. Even though I now had more time to write undisturbed than I had since the start of the course, I found myself staring at a flashing cursor on a blank screen. I was still going to my job at the juice kitchen, diligently labelling bottles and packing up orders. I found the repetitive tasks soothing. Molly complimented me on some weight loss, which she attributed to my new diet of beetroot juice. She came by to pick up a green juice to mix with an avocado for dinner. I raised my eyebrows at Olena after she left and we laughed, but I didn't feel like talking to her about her relationship troubles.

Henderson was the first to arrive and he came to sit next to me. He pulled out his latest piece and told me how long it had taken him just to get something onto the page.

'It sounds strange,' he said, rubbing at the corners of his eyes with the arms of his glasses. 'But this time, I didn't write anything for Sofie. I only did it because I didn't want to let the group down.'

I said that was probably the best way to write, even though he had no responsibility to us to submit any work. But I knew what he meant. Maybe the most useful thing we gained from the course was each other. We were the work, we were the stories. Although we often ignored each other's feedback, we also gave each other space. Space to write and talk about writing with sincerity. When we were together, we were writers, and to take up that identity and to be given the courage to run with it and see how far you could go was the most valuable gift of all.

I said something like this and he nodded. 'Maybe next term I'll choose Robert as my tutor, after all.'

I paused, wondering how to ask him something.

'Sofie's been here since the nineties, right?'

He nodded, tapping his bundle of pages on the table so that they came together in an even pile.

'And the rate of people being published from the course is pretty good. But do we know how many people have dropped out? How many people had a horrible time?'

He frowned at me. 'You can't leave. You're already halfway through. This is the worst part.'

'I'm not thinking about leaving,' I said. 'I was only wondering about talking to students who had already left. I want to know what their experience was of the course, how they dealt with it all, what they thought of Sofie. The way she invites the group back to her house all the time, the way she's so involved. I half thought when we started that she might, you know, sleep with students.'

Henderson laughed. 'Jesus Christ, really?'

'I read something about it online.'

'You can read anything about anyone online.'

I smiled back, half-heartedly. 'So, you don't reckon that ever happens?'

He pushed his glasses up the bridge of his nose. 'I guess it's possible. But I seriously doubt it. Why would anyone in her position risk that kind of reputation?'

'I guess.'

'Also, getting into bed with your students tends to be a traditionally male occupation.'

I nodded, taking a sip of my coffee. 'So is being a bestselling novelist,' I said.

He laughed again at that and then the others arrived at our sticky table. The whole place smelt like ground coffee and lemon cleaner. When we were together as a collective, though we often formed little tribes and split groups, there was always a buzz in the air. Soon we'd be starting on our novels, crossing into uncharted territory. We shared ideas and lamented the difficulty of the work. We shared our frustrations about Sofie's feedback and then repeated the same mantra. She was successful; she knew what she was doing.

The words hung in my head as we made our way to the workshop. I saw Walt arrive just as we all sat down in our seats. He took a desk near the doorway without saying anything. Sofie arrived with a smile, and as though nothing strange had happened in the last few days, took a cheerful sip from her mug – the one that she always had, the one she had left in Walt's room. I felt a lurch to imagine him handing it back.

Walt said very little throughout the class, as Sofie talked about opening scenes in novels. He smiled at Stella when she made a joke about capturing the reader's attention by making women suffer in the opening pages, like in *Jaws*. But as I caught his eye, I could see the joy had drained from his face. His skin dragged across his cheekbones. He ruffled his hair and rubbed the dark circles around his eyes and mumbled something about being too hungover to think about shark attacks.

I stared at the mug as though it was about to explode. Between words and looks, I tried to decipher any kind of dynamic between Walt and Sofie, but I couldn't see anything beyond what I'd always seen: the usual relationship between teacher and student. I couldn't fill in the gaps or conjure up sweet nothings, and I marvelled at the way my imagination failed me.

I hung around at the end of the class as Sofie packed her things away and the others filed out. I felt a desire to speak to Sofie, but wasn't entirely sure what I wanted to say. She clicked the lock on her bag shut and looked up at me. 'Everything all right, Alice?' She looped the strap over her shoulder. I hesitated, searching for the words. Then, as though deliberately prompting me, she picked up her empty mug to put it back in her bag.

'You found your mug.'

She lifted it up to the light. 'Ah, yes, mystery solved.'

'I saw it . . .' I stopped. It all seemed so stupid now I was vocalising it. What did I think had happened, exactly? What was I trying to say to her?

She interrupted me. 'I told Walt how stupid I was. We had a tutorial on campus, and I left it behind. So he said he'd keep it safe for me until our next class.'

I smiled. How easy was that?

'Do you want me to tell you a secret, Alice?' She clutched the mug to her chest like it was a memento from her childhood. She looked almost giddy – to clear the air or to lie? 'One of my old students gave me this mug. She made it, actually. I thought it was so funny all those years ago. I still do. It was a lot more risqué back then of course.' She turned the mug towards me, from side to side, pointing to the painterly spots. 'I sort of like the idea that at least one of us can walk around with our chest out. She later became my wife, of course. It reminds me every day that women truly are the superior sex.'

Her eyes lifted towards the door, and she waved at someone on the outside. She tapped me on the shoulder and said goodbye. 'I can't wait for your next piece, truly. There's no one I enjoy reading more.'

Some days she was like a hurricane, and we were all just living inside her weather.

I spent a few tortured weeks wondering what would happen next. Then, one Tuesday, the next thing happened.

The season had turned cooler, the lake almost frozen over, and in class some people talked about gearing up for an icy dip in the sea that weekend.

I'd managed to pull together a vague plot for the novel that Sofie had encouraged me to write. The deadline for submission was only a few days away. Some of the others were agitated and directionless, lamenting having no ideas or otherwise not being able to pull together their plans, but I felt ready to start.

We were all meeting at one of the campus bars that evening for farewell drinks before Christmas. I'd decided to stay on even though the campus would be deserted. I thought it would give me an uninterrupted period of time to get on with my work. I was looking forward to the silence and not worrying about bumping into Walt at the Union café.

That morning, just as I'd had the thought, Walt was at a table nursing a coffee. He looked as though he'd been hanging around and when he saw me, quickly took a sip and turned a page in his book. I stepped forward in the queue to order my own drink and then stepped over to ask how he was.

'Oh, you know, merry and bright.'

He smiled, but he looked drained and pale. I was concerned for him, but couldn't find a way to say so. We stood there while the milk steamer hissed behind me, waiting for the takeaway cup that would release me from the room. As the steamer got louder, he turned to me in a sort of panic. 'I have to talk to you – now.'

'There's really nothing to say, and I'm finding this whole situation *insane*.'

'It's not what you think,' he kept saying, tapping a teaspoon in the palm of his hand. 'It's really not what you think.'

I stepped out of the way to let another student pass and then turned back to him. 'Okay,' I said, 'how is it not what I think?'

'I could tell you she lost that mug and I was looking after it for her. That could be the end of it.'

I raised my eyebrows sarcastically. 'Well, that's Sofie's story, so at least you're in sync.' He knew as well as I did that that mug never left her sight.

'The thing is,' he told me, 'you wouldn't believe me. You just wouldn't believe me. You probably think it's some illicit affair.' He looked up at the ceiling. 'Oh God, that's probably what she thought. That it was a hopelessly romantic, consensual situation.'

I felt sick. *She*. Sofie.

'It started before I'd even come here. The moment I applied and came for the interview. It's been months.' He screwed his face up. 'It's been going on for months.'

The barista called my name. After collecting my coffee, I lowered my voice and said, 'You've been sleeping together for months?' I could barely get the words out.

He went to grab my arm, but stepped backwards. Some of the frothy milk oozed from the mouth in the plastic lid of my coffee.

'No . . .' he sounded incredulous. 'She's been non-stop. Contacting me all the time. I don't even know how to describe it, what you'd call it. She's been harassing me.'

'And you've been having sex with her?' I hissed.

'No, Alice, you don't understand. The claims she made were on my life, my time. I got in too deep. I slept in her bed, I did everything she told me to: I read her books out loud to her, I got down on my knees and adored her. I . . .' he hesitated, then visibly steeled himself before continuing. 'I shaved her legs in the bath, and cut her toenails, which she collected in a jar. It was weird, obsessive, even romantic, maybe, but there was no sex. Not at first.'

I snorted in disbelief, but he continued, his voice strained and desperate.

'But that wasn't the problem. I had no time to write, but that was the least of it. It was like I'd been robbed of independent thought and action. We even had pet names for each other. That's not a sex thing – she has nicknames for everyone in the class. Henderson is the Undertaker. Beatrice is the Beaver. Grace is Waste of Space.'

I suppressed a twinge of *schadenfreude* at this.

'She calls and messages me almost constantly,' he said, 'so that she's never far away. At first, I was flattered. She told me she'd help me get a book deal. But it all became way too much.'

'What about me?' I asked.

He frowned, uncomprehending.

'What's her name for me?'

'Last week,' he said, as if he hadn't heard my question, 'we stayed up all night, talking and drinking. I fell asleep in bed with her, on top of the bedsheets, clothed, and then . . .' He swallowed. 'I woke up early in the morning to find her on top of me, having sex with me. I grabbed her by the shoulders to push her off and she said I could put my hands on her throat if I liked. I said I didn't want to do any of that, and she said it was better that I did.'

I didn't know what to say. The horrible details were pouring out of him, here in a corner of the cafeteria.

'She started kissing my chest,' he said, 'and I could feel her wet mouth on my nipples, my whole body flinching in response. It was an out-of-body experience, like I couldn't control it. Finally, without hurting her, I managed to push her off me, to the other side of the bed.' His mouth was twisted in misery and self-loathing. 'It was intensely wrong and awful, like finding a clot of hair in your food. But worse than that, so much worse. It was more than something being out of place, off kilter. It was unspeakable. I just can't get the image of her naked body like that out of my mind. It was horrifying.'

He was pink and sweating, and he wouldn't look me in the eye. I got the distinct feeling he'd been rehearsing how to say this and what words he should choose. All I could think was, what a thing to say. He was right, it was like a clot of hair, and now it was lodged in my own mind too.

'I've told her it's over now. It has to be. And you,' he said, looking up at me for the first time. 'I don't want you to get dragged into something you can't get out of. She does have a name for you too, but it's different, because she likes you. She thinks you're it. You're really it.'

I wasn't sure if this was meant to flatter me. I felt like I had walked in on a child rehearsing a play they'd written. I suddenly recalled the man who'd approached Sofie months ago at the bookshop. The way he said her name incredulously. Didn't we all realise how easily forgotten we were? What was our obsession with being special?

I asked what my nickname was. I wanted to leave; I took one step away.

'*Schnecke*. It means snail. She's waiting for you to come out of your shell. You're very talented and she sees it, she . . .' the sentence fell apart as he was saying it and he shook his head. 'You don't believe me, do you?'

I turned towards the exit, yanked the door open and ran out, looking back only once I was far enough away. But he didn't come after me and my name wasn't called. Once I was in my room with the door locked, I sat on the corner of my bed. I loved him. I *thought* I loved him. But he was right. I couldn't believe him.

I thought that would be the end of it, and I could walk out of the door and get on with my life. I could write my book and dismiss the whole mess from my head. But as was always the case with everything concerning Sofie Muller, I knew nothing, nothing, nothing.

The second phase

Posted by G0rmlessVidal

Sexual harassment at uni – looking for advice.

It started fairly innocently. My tutor on my Master's course used to email me book recommendations or films she'd watched that she thought I might like (and related to my work). But when I started replying, it became a near-constant stream of communication and personal invitations to her house.

Naively, I went over one evening. She plied me with wine and touched my leg. It was really uncomfortable, but she kept telling me how she thought my dissertation would be the best in the year and she could help me find a great job after the course if I wanted one.

I went to the bathroom and when I came back, she was undressing in the living room. She told me she wanted me to check a mole on her back. When I had a look, she asked me to give her a massage. I felt I couldn't say no, but once I started, she was groaning in pleasure.

Since then, whenever I see her, she wants me to touch her and lie in bed with her. She emails me incredibly romantic messages and gets angry when I don't reply in the same tone. It's all done under the guise of us forming a close working partnership, and she runs the entire course, so it's hard to say no. I want to graduate and do well, but I'm worried about the logical conclusion to all this.

What should I do?

35 comments

One

Jo

When people asked her how she met her wife, she tried not to say it had been because of Control-F. She had found that out later, how Sofie would choose which students to admit to her exclusive writing course. She would open up the folder of applications from the admissions office and search her own name. Jo had seen her do it. Control-F: Sofie Muller. The students who specifically mentioned her in their cover letter got an interview. There were a lot of them, too. The promise of access to a semi-famous novelist invites a lot of attention.

That's how Jo had felt, in the nineties, when all she wanted to do was write and there was one great course to make that happen. That if she just had access to someone like Sofie, she'd be sorted. The great barrier between herself and the thing she wanted to do was just the right person. She only needed one person who mattered to read her work and she'd be fine. She decided that was Sofie and told her so when she applied to the course. She might have even used the word genius. She laughed at that now.

In fact, she was always laughing at the idea of Sofie until she received one of her plaintive emails. It happened every few months after a period of silence. Suddenly Sofie would miss her and it would all come pouring out. Did Jo remember the time they were in Porto together? Sofie wished they were there now. She had a headache, a dreadful one, and all she could think of were Jo's hands soothing her scalp, her head in Jo's lap. Would she like that?

Sofie made it impossible. They'd been divorced for over a decade, but with Sofie there was no concept of linear time. There were only the people who orbited around her, and once you were in, you were stuck for good. Jo had tried to get out of it. People used to ask her if she minded being married to someone famous, whose face showed up in the newspaper. Someone who ended up on judging panels and television programmes. She remembered how they used to lean towards her at cocktail parties and tell her: all the men are after Sofie. Isn't it amazing? That all the men would get down and kiss her feet if she asked them to.

Jo would scoff at that. People couldn't conceive of desire that had no place for men. They couldn't even imagine it. They couldn't believe that if the most handsome men wanted you, you could possibly want a woman. And a young one at that. But she had been beautiful at that age, hadn't they noticed? People told Jo she was striking. All they meant was that she was living in that window of time when your face always looked as ripe as a peach, and your body as smooth as an apple, but you were innocent to the power that gave you.

The good thing about marrying your professor was the prestige that came with it. She'd seen it happen to other women, just like her. With male professors mostly. They'd pick you out, leave their partner for you, and you'd be ordained. Everyone would gasp and wouldn't say: it's because she's the most charming, the most beautiful. No, they would all whisper about how it must mean you were the most intellectually gifted. So, she had the beauty and Sofie gave her the smarts.

Now she thought those people knew nothing.

When she was with Sofie, she used to think about winning the lottery. She spent hours planning how she'd spend the money and where she'd live. She felt better and safer in this imagining. She used to tell Sofie about it: the library room she'd have; the pink wallpaper, the floor-to-ceiling bookshelves.

That conversation became a permanent fixture in their repertoire, especially on a bad day. It amazed Jo that even though Sofie seemingly had everything, she could empathise with the idea of wanting more. In fact, she was more forthcoming about the things she wanted than Jo had been. Sofie might have a house, but lots of people she knew had better ones. If she won the lottery, she'd buy a Modernist spectacle with glass walls and a swimming pool.

Neither of them ever played the lottery, but that was almost the point.

If Jo had been so inclined, she might have made some crass remark about winning the lottery by being with Sofie. But she knew Sofie would have hated that, and part of the fun was imagining things that would never come to be.

Jo often longed to call Sofie up during a period of silence and ask her if she remembered some moment like this from their lives together that would play in her head on repeat. She longed to have her feelings validated by the one person who always refused to do it.

Wasn't that what love was about?

The day she got the email, she was walking along the river in Norwich, while the sun was still low in the sky. There was frost on the ground and the wet pad of her feet reminded her of time spent by Sofie's swimming lake. For years after she moved there, Sofie insisted that they had to swim all year round for their vitality. Even though they'd been broken up for a long time by then and sometimes didn't talk for months, when she messaged to ask her for a swim, Jo would go without thinking. That was the power of Sofie.

The last time she went, she hoped the day in late summer would cheer her up, knowing Sofie would be in a good mood with a new crop of students just starting at the university. They had lunch in the garden, watching the water glisten in front of them. Sofie was cutting her tomato slices into quarters, measuring carefully what she would put in her mouth. She was always like that and it irritated Jo, her affected sense of glamour. You're a writer! She wanted to scream sometimes, but, in a way, she didn't believe even that.

Sofie told Jo that she needed to be careful with her dairy consumption, as Jo stuffed a mozzarella slice into her mouth. She asked Sofie why she'd say that after offering her cheese.

'I didn't ask for cheese,' Jo said, 'you were the one who gave it to me.'

Sofie shrugged. 'Precisely. I wanted to see if you'd have the restraint to refuse.' She told Jo she wouldn't be young forever and things that come from a cow were particularly ageing.

'But I'm still young now,' Jo pointed out, spearing another piece of mozzarella with her fork, her lips slick with olive oil. 'I've got twenty years on you, remember.'

Sofie was in good spirits. She wasn't rattled by this comment as she normally would be. Instead, she brushed a hand over her perfectly dyed hair and laughed as though it were really funny. She looked over the lake and Jo couldn't help but think she was beautiful. Sofie knew it too, that was part of the charm. But it still seemed effortless and not of her own choosing. Like she was the one being taken for a ride and not the other way round.

The sun was beating down on her plate and Jo longed to get in the water. In a sense, she'd only come here for the sweet consumption of the cold lake. She couldn't wait for the gasp of freshness to swallow up her body. She hated sitting here, pretending they were such good friends. Jo was getting angrier by the minute, just looking at her, and Sofie could tell.

This was one of her tricks. Make it seem like she'd invited her friend to a nice lunch by the lake and make it seem as though Jo was being difficult. But she knew, she *knew* something was off. Sofie had brought Jo here to gloat. *Ah,* Jo thought. She's done it again.

Jo dropped her fork on her plate so that it clattered, and Sofie turned sharply to look at her.

'We're not together any more. You can't tell me what I should be eating.'

Sofie smiled: another win.

'It's just a bit of advice, that's all.'

Jo got up from the table and stood on the wooden decking that surrounded the lake. She'd slipped into this pool so many times, she couldn't count. She put a hand on the metal rail of the steps.

'Don't you want to get changed first? I can lend you something if you've forgotten.'

Jo could tell Sofie was resisting the urge to add that nothing of hers would fit.

'Men would never sit around and talk about cheese,' she said. 'They'd think it was pointless.'

'I never said I wanted to talk about cheese.'

Jo slipped a foot under the dark water, holding on to the rail for support. Her body eased in response. It was good to be by the water. That's why she hadn't left the area, even years afterwards. It felt right.

'Who is she, then?' Jo said, almost without thinking, not looking back at Sofie. She hadn't wanted to give in to Sofie's good mood, but she did want to know. She sometimes felt so sorry for them that she couldn't sleep. In a way it was like feeling sorry for herself.

'Who's who?'

Without turning round Jo could tell that Sofie was delighted. She could sense her stretching out her legs and taking a sip of her wine, could hear the glass clinking in deep satisfaction.

Jo arranged her face in a smile and turned to her.

'Are you going to be coy about it?'

Sofie shrugged. She was wearing a silk kimono, the kind that could either be a dressing gown or a whole outfit. 'I might be.'

It reminded Jo of all the times she'd delighted at mornings where she could slip a hand under the lapel of Sofie's dressing gown and feel her bare skin. How she'd gently ease the tie open like a secret that was only hers.

'I suppose it's someone with a lot of promise?'

Sofie seemed to think seriously about this.

'Yes, you're right. They do have a lot of promise.'

Jo sat down on the edge of the deck now, putting both her legs in the water, and Sofie came to stand beside her. Jo looked up and Sofie put a hand on Jo's head as though she was trying to initiate intimacy with a child.

'Don't you want to swim?' Sofie asked.

Jo kicked her legs in the water.

'I want you to tell me about her.'

Sofie laughed.

'You can't be jealous.' She went back to the table, picked up her glass. 'You left me, Jocasta. Remember?'

It was true, she had. From this exact house, too, before it was remodelled into a Modernist cube. She left one weekend just before Sofie went on a press tour for her latest novel. She took one suitcase. She thought it would be easier, nothing to fight over. But Sofie didn't want stuff, she wanted her.

Sofie had found Jo's new address easily, too easily. She turned up and rang the doorbell without stopping for hours. She begged for forgiveness. She screamed through the door. She told her she'd never write another word without Jo. She screamed this, too. Jo wanted to shout back: I hope so. But she knew it wouldn't take long for there to be another Jo, another little writer. The world was filled with them.

She wrote one novel once, didn't she? It had been the thing she wrote with Sofie on the course. It had even won a little prize. But she knew the one thing Sofie always told her was true: if she left, there'd be no going back. She'd never have a writing career again. Sofie would have made her a star, and she was throwing it all away. Sofie said a lot of things that weren't true back then, but Jo knew that statement meant something. Sofie was a gatekeeper. She could make things happen.

Jo remembered packing that ratty old suitcase. She put her books inside, a couple of paperbacks. She left all the new clothes Sofie had bought her. She left their whole life. When Sofie had stood on her doorstep and rung that bell, for hours, on different days over the course of a few months, it would have been easy to open the door and go back. It was only years later, when she thought Sofie had forgotten all about her, that she started to miss her. She missed feeling singular and special.

Sofie accepted her back readily. They tried again, for a few months, but this time Sofie got bored, or pretended to. Jo was older now, less interesting. Her writing career had indeed died a death. Sofie said she could do her whole life without Jo now, but they should remain friends.

'Only my mother calls me Jocasta,' Jo said. Sofie was trying to rile her. 'And I'm not jealous.' She got up, her legs dripping, then sat back down at the table and asked for more wine.

Sofie gladly poured her another glass.

'Actually,' she said, refilling her own at the same time, 'It's not at all what you think it is, what your small mind is suggesting.' She seemed happy, and productive in her happiness. Maybe soon there'd even be a new novel.

Jo took a large sip.

'Oh?'

'This year,' said Sofie, 'my star student is a boy. A man, even. He's been incredibly receptive to my tutelage and I'm sure he'll turn out to be a fascinating writer. Under my instruction, he could be the next big thing. Which wouldn't exactly harm the reputation of the course.'

Jo nodded.

'Sure.' It wasn't unusual for Sofie to have a star student. It wasn't even unusual for that star to be a man. She felt a little relieved. She lifted up her glass of wine for Sofie to tap hers against. 'Well, cheers to your work. It must all feel worth it when you find someone talented.'

'It does.' Sofie winked at her. 'It still does.'

Jo felt almost warm towards her. It wasn't like how it was back then. Sofie had matured. She was old, even. Jo was sure the last time they talked that Sofie had had a date with a doctor, a woman at least in her forties.

It was as though a bad fright from a stranger had turned out to be nothing more than a greeting from a familiar friend. She said, 'Actually, I will swim after all.'

Six months later, Jo received an email. She was walking along the river and sat down on a bench, just for a moment, checking her phone to see whether her colleagues had got back to her about an ad campaign. That was the kind of thing she did now. Creative concepts, slogans, social media copy. Words that were short, pithy. It was still fiction, but had nothing to do with the novel. She liked that.

Instead, a new email had popped up that was different from the rest. It was a name she didn't recognise. She read it twice and then reminded herself to take a breath. There was always talk about Sofie, about one thing or another, wasn't there? This was just another of those things: an imagined grievance, magicked out of nowhere, something Jo had nothing to do with.

But somehow, she still felt caught up in it all, as though she could stop the train from crashing. Even years after Sofie screamed through Jo's door. The neighbours had come round the next morning and asked her if she was okay. She'd had to explain. It was her ex-wife; she wasn't happy about the situation. She needed time to get used to it, that was all.

Even after all that, somehow the orbit remained, the natural way things moved around Sofie. Jo had been flippant about it that hot summer day: glib, happy, relieved.

It was true that being with Sofie felt like playing a lottery, and most days, she'd make sure you lost. But you were always scrambling around for that winning ticket that you'd swear you once grasped in your hands – clutched between desperate fingers, rolled up into a ball, discarded in a drawer, in the glove compartment, in your jeans pocket, incinerated in the tumble dryer – the one you could never quite seem to find again.

It felt like that still, years later: the effect they had on each other was fatal. It was hard to get away from the things they'd done together.

A woman walking her dog along the river glanced over. Jo shifted on the bench. The dog wagged its tail, brushing up against the cold air, a wet pant visible from its mouth. From the outside, the day looked simple.

Jo put her phone away and kept walking.

Two

Alice

The campus grew quiet over the Christmas holidays. The place was eerily abandoned and the wind threw itself around the staggered buildings I'd grown to call my home. I told my parents it was busy still, and I would be having Christmas Day with a friend. In reality, only a few of us stayed on, wandering around the corridors, paperbacks in one hand and coffees in another. We walked the wide green spaces that stretched out from our living quarters and hunched over laptops in the library.

Walt was one of the few who had stayed behind. The next time I saw him, a small group of us had gone to a local pub quiz. We couldn't correctly guess Isaac Asimov's date of birth and we were trailing behind after ten questions. He turned up late, drunk, and immediately identified the name for the plastic on the end of shoelaces. Beatrice asked him how he knew the answer as she drew over the face of who we thought was Brigitte Macron (picture round).

'I don't know,' he shrugged, 'I just do.'

She told him he was being smug, especially because he was clearly already a few pints down.

'I could leave if you like.' He took another sip from his beer and licked the foam from his top lip. He looked across at me and I pretended to be listening intently to the quizmaster.

Beatrice gave me a sideways look.

'Walt should stay, we might be in with a chance now.' She cleared her throat and widened her eyes at me.

'Right,' I said, picking up my warm glass of wine, nodding. 'Of course you should stay.'

'The answer is *Vilnius*,' he said.

I hadn't heard the question but nodded in agreement. He laughed at something Beatrice said and I felt heartsore. I couldn't help it. I desperately wanted him to leave me alone but at the same time to only laugh at things *I* said.

'Alice thought Minsk was a type of fur coat,' Walt smirked.

'I did not. And what's that got to do with Latvia anyway?'

'Lithuania.'

'That's what I meant. I knew it was an L one.'

'Thank God I arrived when I did.' He downed the rest of his pint.

I raised an eyebrow to reprimand his drinking and he pointed at my half-full wine glass. 'Time for another?'

I shrugged in agreement and then excused myself to go to the bathroom. I sat on the toilet and listed all the reasons in my head that I shouldn't talk to Walt. Number one, he was possibly a delusional, self-obsessed liar. Then I thought about the way he always looked at me. I had to remind myself of number two: laughs at his own jokes. Thinks people have a good sense of humour only if they laugh too.

But – it only seemed a few weeks ago that we would sit and do crosswords together. He had touched my knee while I told him that *addicting* wasn't a word, and he told me it was. This, this is addicting, he said, and then he stroked my hair.

Number three, and most importantly, he didn't love me. Hadn't ever, would never. It had been fun, was now just confusing, and not in a fun way. Also, when I pointed out to him *addicting* was an Americanism, he wouldn't believe me until he'd googled it.

But – his face.

I left the bathroom and he intercepted me on the way back to the table. He was holding our drinks like a peace offering. I took the glass of wine and thanked him.

'Stop being so polite, Alice.'

'I can't help it.' I looked towards our table. We'd missed several questions.

'Even when you hate me, you still tell me you'll get the next round.'

'It's the done thing.' I waited for him to step aside but he blinked at me, like he was seeing through a fog. Then he took my arm and pulled me round the corner to a nook with a fireplace and frayed leather sofa. I started to protest but let him lead me. He put his drink down on the mantel.

'So, you do hate me then.' He was starting to slur his words, so he overcorrected, enunciating each one slowly.

'Please, let's not do this. You're drunk.' I tried to say it kindly.

'But you let me talk to you. You let me buy you a drink. Even though you hate me and I've had too many, and who knows what I'll do next.'

'I'm easily persuaded. My dad used to call me a marketer's dream – I'd buy anything. As an undergraduate I always ate the branded jam and ketchup, even when I realised it was no different from the regular stuff and double the price.'

'What does this have to do with anything?'

'It works the same way with people, too.'

'So, what? You fall for people easily?' I looked down at my wine glass. 'What else is there to do?' He had a point. 'Better to fall for checked jam jars and condiments that punch up a sandwich.' He lifted his beer in the air for exaggeration and the liquid slopped over the side of the glass. 'Better that than falling for a theory or doctrine, or something really terrible, like the Royal Family.'

'Or men who make you laugh, who have a bit of whimsy.'
'Ah.'
I tried to take a step past him, but he blocked me.
'I was just a game to you,' I said.
He shook his head.
'No. Sorry.' He rubbed his face and steadied himself. 'The truth is, I was completely overwhelmed. I've never felt like that before. Overwhelmed by Sofie, I mean. You were the only thing that helped pull me out of it.'
'Do you love her?'
He laughed.
'It isn't funny!'
'No,' he said. 'It's the grim kind of laughter. The kind you do at a funeral when you don't know what to say.'
I looked at him blankly. 'I don't know what to say either.' I couldn't tell him my feelings were hurt. I wondered if he'd even remember this conversation tomorrow.
He took my wine glass out of my hand and put it on the mantel. He went to take my hands, but I folded my arms.
'I don't want you to leave me,' he said. 'I want you to stay and help me.' I didn't say anything. 'It's hard for men to ask for help, isn't it? But look, I'm doing it.' He pointed at his chest exaggeratedly. 'I want you to stay with me, be with me. I want you to believe me. I don't know what else I'm meant to do now.'
It was true there was power in asking directly for what you wanted. But I just wanted love – and to write a book. I came here to write a book.
'Look, I just need someone to be on my side.' After a pause, he reached out and touched my shoulder – his fingers light on the edge of my collarbone, like he was peeling back the paper from a gift with the utmost care. I thought the touch was designed to tell me something. I wanted to hold him, wanted him to tell me it was all a misunderstanding and everything could go on as it was before. He

pulled me in towards him and for a moment, I let him, leaning my cheek against the soft wool of his jumper.

'No,' I said. 'I can't now. You've ruined it and I don't know what to think. I'm scared.'

He wrapped his arm tighter around me and rested his chin on my head. He sighed. 'We're all scared, Alice, that's the point.' He rubbed my back. 'You're right though,' he said into my hair. 'Falling in love is the easy part. It's the part that happens after that's difficult.'

'I can't,' I said. It was easy to be with him, as he was practised at accommodating the wants and needs of other people. It was easy to touch him, too. But I had my list, I had my reasons. Number four, he always said the right thing a little too late. 'Not now, not now,' I said, quietly. It made me feel nauseous thinking about how he had pawed over me, the smell of his skin so close to mine. I cringed thinking about the way he'd kissed my face, my stomach, all the while with a bigger conquest in mind. In how many conversations had he fawned over me, touching my thigh while I longed to slip under him, before he turned to his phone?

'The whole time you were with me,' I said, 'you were really with her. And I just thought it was your overprotective mother constantly lighting up your phone. But that was all a lie too.'

He released me from his grip.

'Nothing I told you about my mother has ever been a lie. I just didn't know how to explain it. It wasn't like that. It wasn't.'

I couldn't tell him the truth. I cared about him a lot more than jam jars. But the whole time, he'd been enthralled by someone else. And now, he wanted me to abandon my work with Sofie, my writing, the one thing that brought me joy.

'I'm sorry I can't help you,' I said. 'I have to think about myself, too.' I wanted to tell him how much he'd hurt me. That I had to let go of all my fantastical ideas about us, which would take time and effort.

Instead, keeping my voice neutral, I asked him if he was going home for Christmas.

'So that's it, then?' he said. Over the microphone, the quizmaster asked the teams to name the director of the FBI who shared his last name with a US president. I could see Walt's brain whirring. He picked up his beer and said, 'J. Edgar Hoover.'

'Right,' I said. 'And Henry Hoover.'

'Not Henry Hoover, Alice. Herbert Hoover.'

I picked up my wine glass and took a big gulp. 'Don't tell the others.'

He smiled and for a moment I forgot what had happened. Then he shook his head like he was shaking off a bad dream, and went back to the table. I slipped out without saying goodbye to the others, without looking back at him.

Number five: broke my heart a little. Wouldn't let me break his heart back.

I went to the juice kitchen in the afternoons during the break and carefully labelled hundreds of bottles with their best before date. The products only lasted three days and I wondered who was doing a juice fast before Christmas, but the orders had hardly died down. I arrived early before all the fresh juice had been made and watched the women on the cold press machines. Buckets of spinach and freshly cut pineapple were passed through pressing bags, before a lever was pulled to clamp down on the produce. Out ran what felt like a disappointingly small amount of product that was collected for Olena to mix into different flavours.

Only Olena knew all the different quantities for each recipe. She wouldn't even show me the sheet of paper she kept them on. It was why she got such a good hourly rate, she told me. Once I'd finished labelling empty bottles ready to be filled and put into cool bags, I went into the back office to organise the deliveries. I watched Olena from the window that looked out onto the kitchen. She was diligent with her pouring and mixing, referring to her sheet's arithmetic often. She seemed to enjoy the quiet solitude of her task. While the other women removed their hair nets and cleaned the machines to get ready to leave for the day, her work would continue into the evening.

I typed the customers' addresses into the system, booking the different couriers that would take the deliveries to their destinations. I tried to be careful and concentrated in my tasks, but the more distracted I was by my real work, the writing, the more stupid mistakes I made and had to start over. I imagined Kiara Roberts drinking her three-day juice cleanse in her Knightsbridge flat, while Sarah Olufsson devoured her series of kale drinks in Cambridge. I typed their addresses into Google and wondered what would possess someone to spend hundreds of pounds on drinks that removed the best part of fruit and vegetables, leaving a bag of pulp behind. When I arrived in the afternoons, I would watch bin after bin of vegetable remnants discarded as each dribble of juice was collected.

I picked up my silver Sharpie and wrote a thank-you note to a Benjamin Oatley on a printed card. *Enjoy your juice cleanse!* The pen smudged and I had to rewrite it. I rolled through the orders like this, occasionally stopping to watch Olena performing her own mundane task.

I took out another card and tapped the Sharpie on the table. I was almost done, and I pressed the nib into the paper. *Dear Sofie.* I looked back at the spreadsheet. There was a one-day juice cleanse going out this evening, plus an extra spicy shot and two cashew milks. For Sofie Muller. The pen wobbled in my hand. I was sure I hadn't told Sofie in our tutorials that I worked here, it was just one of those strange coincidences.

I looked at Olena, who gestured at me that she'd finished filling the bottles. They were ready to be packed up and sent off. She took off her hair net and came and sat next to me at the table.

'I am glad the day is over,' she said, 'but now I don't want to go home. I will wait for you while you finish packing the bottles.'

I grabbed the printed sheet of orders and we went back into the kitchen. When I put Sofie's bag together, I looked at each bottle carefully, ensuring the labels were straight and the juice looked right. They were perfect.

I asked Olena what was wrong, expecting her to lament more time that she'd spent with Alan. Instead, she told me she'd been doing some digging on her husband.

'I just felt so frustrated, it felt like the right thing to do. I knew something was different about him. He was on his phone all the time, smiling at it like an idiot. I suspected something straight away. But people always say: if you go looking for something, you'll find it.'

I zipped up another bag and labelled it with the right address.

'And did you?'

She leant against the fridge.

'Of course. While he was sleeping, I got onto his laptop. I looked through his emails, his Amazon account, his internet search history. Nothing.'

I nodded, slipping another set of juices into a bag and ticking the order off my sheet.

'Then I got hold of his phone one night, and again there was nothing there. Only texts from his mum and friends.'

'I mean, *you* have a burner phone to call Alan on . . .'

'Exactly.' She tapped the lid of one of the juices. 'But in the end, it was more stupid than that. I searched the entire house and his van for a second phone, anything. There was nothing. So I went back to his phone and looked through his messages again. I read all the messages from his mother. Only they weren't from his mother. They were very sexual, which surprised me – I thought he just didn't feel that way any more. I do not know who this woman is, but now I have proof.'

I could tell she was angry. She folded her arms across her chest and picked at one of her nails.

'These things, the kind of things they wrote to each other, should only be for a husband and wife.'

I didn't want to point out that she had been having her own extra-marital activities, but she saw the look on my face.

'It's different with him,' she said. 'When we got married, he told me he'd love me until the day he died.'

'And what did you say to him?'

She smiled, looking off into the distance. I could imagine Olena, younger, full of fight. 'I told him my mother was making me do it.' Her face dropped and she bit one of her nails again. 'And he said that was okay. It was how all the best marriages started.'

She smiled at me, weakly.

'It'll be okay,' I told her. 'If anything, this gives you more choice. You can leave your husband now and not feel guilty.'

But she just shook her head.

'That's the thing,' she said. 'It doesn't change anything. I have to go on with my life and pretend it didn't even happen.'

I asked her about Alan, how she'd been feeling about him. She exhaled dismissively. 'They're all the same, aren't they? They have their fun and then they go to bed early, rolling over and snoring endlessly. They need a good night's sleep for all the pointless shit they get up and do the next day.' She clapped her hands together as though remembering something, went over to one of the commercial fridges and pulled out two one-litre bottles of juice that were more than three days old. 'I can't use it any more, so you should take it.'

'Thanks,' I said. 'Everyone has their own story, you know, of how things happen. Maybe you should just come out and ask him. See what he has to say.'

She pulled out her two phones from her pocket, holding them together in one hand. 'But then I'd have to listen to his answer.'

'Even so, sometimes it's better to hear the truth.'

Olena laughed at that, walking away.

'You're right that everyone has their own story, and that's what you fill your little notebooks with.' She tapped her brick phone. 'But none of us ever get the whole truth.'

After handing over the bags of juice to the courier, I kept one back.

When Sofie opened her front door, she didn't seem particularly surprised to see me. She took her bag of juices gratefully and then ushered me in for a drink. She told me she thought I'd mentioned that I worked at the local juicery. She hadn't expected a hand-delivered service, but sometimes things just work out nicely, don't they?

She offered me a glass of sloe gin, making a joke about her juice diet, which would have to be delayed.

I shrugged.

'If there's fruit in the gin, it probably won't be any worse for you than the juice. We have customers calling all the time asking for the calorie content, but Molly has given me strict instructions never to disclose them.'

I stood awkwardly at her kitchen island, one hand on the terrazzo slab. Everything was so clean and beautiful, it made sense that she would be the kind of person to order a stylish, chunky bottle of juice that didn't really benefit her in any way.

'I think it must be because they're full of sugar,' I continued. 'I'm not sure there's much difference between an apple and kale juice and a can of Coke, just so you know.'

She laughed at that, carefully pouring the gin into cut glass tumblers. 'I thought I'd try it, at least.'

She certainly looked like someone who ate her vegetables. Her skin was unblemished and she was enviably slim. Even though it was late in the evening, she still looked put together in silk trousers and a T-shirt that was probably worth more than all the work I'd done that day. Her hair was up as it usually was, a neat silk headband around her forehead. I looked down at my trainers squeaking on her parquet flooring and felt sweat bloom on my chest. As she replaced the stopper on her bottle of gin, her perfectly polished nails squeezing it into place, I thought about how horrified Walt had been by her body. It was hard to imagine him thinking this, mostly because everything about her was elegant and pristine. I was sure that even naked she would look better than a woman twenty years younger.

We sat down on the sofa opposite the kitchen island, and I looked at the dark glass of her folding doors, hoping to catch a glimpse of her swimming lake. All I could see were our own reflections.

'It's late in the year for you to still be here,' she said.

'I need to do a few extra shifts,' I said. 'And I thought I'd get more writing done if I stayed on.'

She smiled. 'It's admirable that you're making the juice alongside your university work.'

'Oh,' I said, 'I don't actually make the juice.'

She looked disappointed.

'But you like the work?'

I thought about it.

'It's okay, but there never seems an end to it. There's no limit to how much cucumber people will drink, and Molly doesn't really care how late we all have to stay at the kitchen.'

'Ah, so you're the one getting squeezed.' She laughed at her own little joke.

'Do you enjoy your job?' I asked her.

'Well, it's the students that keep me going. That might surprise some people,' she said, 'but when you're always reading new work by talented people, the inspiration is always there.'

The sloe gin had caught up to my face and I beamed at her, feeling a damp heat around my cheeks. It was nice to hear that we weren't just a piece of admin to get through, but a genuine pleasure. I wanted to ask if she felt that way even about people like Henderson and Grace.

Instead, I looked at the bookshelf closest to us. I hadn't grown up in a house with more than one bookcase. I had thought a house full of books would look and smell like a library, stale and reverential. But here they were, objects to delight in and use. I noted a shelf in front of us that was full of her students' work.

She followed my gaze. 'I like to look at them when I come through here every day. It reminds me, when I'm knee-deep in bureaucracy, that it's all worth it. In fact, I've got something you might like – come with me.'

I put my glass down and followed her upstairs, treading lightly on the wide staircase. I felt like she trusted me, and it was a good feeling. I'd been upstairs in her house before, but of course she didn't know that. I wondered if we'd turn into the room I'd been in before, but the door was shut. Instead, we walked along to a room with floral wallpaper and clothes thrown on the bed. This must be the one she slept in.

She told me to excuse the mess and then grabbed a book from her nightstand. I recognised it as one of her own novels. The cover had flowers on it, like a still life oil painting.

'I think this might help with your story,' she said, handing it to me.

I flipped it over in my hands and marvelled at the pages of words she'd brought into existence. It happened to be one of the few novels of hers I hadn't read.

'It was one of the first books I ever wrote,' she said. 'When everything felt difficult and awful. But it's about a marriage, and the protagonist is similar to yours in some ways I think.'

I remembered seeing this novel in bookshops everywhere when I was young. It had been held up as a prominent feminist work. It was hard to imagine that she was a real person, standing in front of me. I thanked her for it. She smiled at me and I waited for her to signal that it was time to leave.

Instead, she pointed at the mess of clothes on her bed.

'I'm getting rid of a few things.' She picked up a shirt with pearl buttons. 'In case there's anything you wanted?'

I wished I still had my glass with me for something to occupy my hands. The air in the room smelt like freesias, decadent and heavy.

'Oh no, I couldn't.'

She looked me up and down, and tittered slightly, as though she was pleased I was being bashful.

'Come on, you can try on anything you like. I love giving my clothes away to people who'll actually wear them.' She picked up a jacket and I saw the designer label stitched neatly in its collar. My heart leapt in my throat at the idea of having it in my possession. I'd never owned anything like it. It would've cost me a month's worth of juice-labelling. I reached out a hand to touch it, suddenly worried the arms would be too tight. I felt the soft wool between my fingers. Sofie looked at me and smiled.

'Go on, try it on. We're about the same size, no?'

I knew she was being polite. Aside from anything else she was at least three inches taller than me. But I pulled off my sweater and put an arm through the sleeve, delighted that it was lined with soft silk. My fingers rasped against it, but she helped me to lift it in place over my shoulders, and it fit. I opened my arms out to her for approval.

'It looks perfect,' she said. She pushed on a door in the far wall, and it opened onto a room at least double the size of my own at university. Fitted clothes rails lined the walls. There was a velvet chair in one corner and an island with a marble top, which displayed small golden dishes of jewellery. Along the edges of each open wardrobe were rows and rows of handbags and shoes, neatly displayed as though she regularly had visitors here. There was a tray of perfumes, the kind you couldn't find in a pharmacy. The lighting was dim, with heavy curtains hung across the window.

I didn't know what to say. It was the most beautiful thing I'd ever seen in real life.

She smiled at me, a hand on my immaculately stitched shoulder, and gestured towards an enormous gilded mirror, but I didn't want to look at myself just yet. Until I was in the picture, everything about the place was perfect. I'd never known anyone who had the money or inclination to organise the clothes they wore as though they were precious artifacts. I'd never seen a whole room full of clothes outside of a department store. It was quiet and peaceful. I wanted to run a hand along the rails and press the points of each pair of shoes.

I stepped into the line of my own reflection and tucked my hair behind my ears. I looked taller, more put together. I looked like someone with potential.

I felt I understood the care she'd taken to arrange her things in this way. Life felt better when everything had its own little place. What I mean is, I knew this room gave her a sense of order, and each day she could come here and decide who she wanted to be. It was a good feeling, one that was contagious and full of possibility.

I suppose that was why, when she encouraged me to try on a whole pile of clothes, I didn't feel embarrassed to undress in front of her, and I didn't ask her to leave.

Rebecca Sarah Ley

October, 2018

My dearest Jocasta,

I am quietly desperate to see you again. Sometimes when I don't, it feels as though our entire life together never existed and I'm okay with it. Other times, I am overwhelmed by a crushing melancholy because I cannot simply stroke your hair and tell you what I had for lunch.

Anyway, come over for tea this week? I hate it when you ignore me. You know it makes me obsess about every small thing I did or said. You can't ignore a handwritten letter. The written word is sacred.

Or, even better, I'll cook you dinner. I promise to make you anything you want and you can have all the cheese you like. Nothing is off the table, sweet Jocasta of mine!

All my love,

Sofie

From: Jill.Frank@thetimes.co.uk
To: Jocasta.franklin@49agency.co.uk
Date: 18 December 2018, 11:58

Subject: Interview request

Dear Jocasta,

I hope you don't mind me contacting you. I'm a journalist currently investigating a series of worrying allegations of misconduct relating to the writer and academic Sofie Muller.

As her ex-partner (and ex-student for that matter), I thought it worth reaching out to you to see if you'd be interested in having an off-the-record chat.

If the investigation goes further, I will be writing an in-depth article surrounding these claims, and I'm sure you'd agree it's best to hear views from all sides.

Below is the best contact info to get me on. I'd appreciate you letting me know either way.

Thanks in advance,

Jill

Three

Jo

At Christmas, Jo tried not to think about her novel. Sometimes people would ask her about it and she'd shrug away the questions. But, that afternoon in Norwich, for whatever reason, it was laid out on a table in an independent bookshop. She'd walked in without expecting anything unusual, admiring the twinkling lights and paper decorations, hoping to find a doorstop of a book to get her through the holidays.

It made sense that so close to the university there'd be a table of alumni works from Sofie's course, but she was surprised hers had been deemed significant enough to make the cut. It still shocked her to see her name on a cover: Jocasta Franklin. There had been books far more successful than hers, people Sofie had nurtured into immense talents. That was a talent in and of itself: being able to spot something no one else saw and tease the golden thread out of their writing.

The table also had a pile of Sofie's own books, a seemingly endless number that had won prize after prize. Even her first few were still reprinted regularly. Sofie used to laugh when the royalty cheques came in. She said it was like being congratulated for something you'd forgotten you'd even done. 'It's free money!' she'd say, high on her own delight, and then she'd say because it was free and not from the daily torture inflicted on her at the university, they had to spend it on something fun. A new pair of shoes, a necklace.

Jo thought this was frivolous, and told her so. But when Sofie bought her gifts during their marriage, it was hard to refuse. Jo had grown up in a small house in East London, where the stained carpets were a dismal shade of plum and the orange wallpaper was always peeling. She'd never thought anything of it until one of her friends at university had told her that her clothes smelt like damp. She didn't know what they meant, and when she went back to her room and sniffed them, she couldn't smell a thing.

When Sofie invited her into her immense house and then, later, bought her clothes that were not only fresh but also expensive, it was hard to say no. She told her mother she wouldn't come back to London. She couldn't stand the way your snot turned black on the Tube, the grim smell of rubbish everywhere. She didn't want to admit she'd find it hard to come back to that small house that she knew would feel wet and sickly as soon as she opened the door.

She used to walk around Sofie's house as it had been then: red brick with polished dark window frames. Sofas upholstered in Designers Guild fabrics and a range cooker. She used to marvel at how neat and new the carpet seemed, never tripping her up along its edges, not frayed where it met the skirting board. She'd walk around and look at the white painted walls, the antique Japanese prints hung with deliberate care. She decided she'd never leave. She never wanted to go back to dark spots in corners and the sound of scurrying rats in the walls.

Jo was reminded of that newness when she saw her novel on the table. It was just as magical as it had ever been. It pained her to look at it. She picked it up. Sofie's quote still stood out on the cover. She had once been a 'bold new voice'.

A woman brushed past her and said, 'Oh! If you're on the fence about that one, you should just buy it. It's sparse and dark and brilliant.'

The woman was wearing a red coat that was too large for her frame, and Jo found herself doubting she'd be the best arbiter of opinion until she told Jo she'd read every book on the table.

'This one's the best,' she said, indicating Sofie's book, *A Bird Came Down*. 'She's always brilliant, of course.'

That hurt Jo even more. She'd meant to thank the woman, tell her she appreciated her going out of her way to recommend something to Jo. But instead, she dropped her novel back on the table, stammered something about an appointment, and left the shop.

Walking back out onto the cobbled street, she couldn't help but think about what it had been like to write. Her first and only published novel. Getting to the end had been a feat in and of itself, it had felt lifechanging. She had realised, at some point: I can do this.

It never became easier the more she did it, but the fog of early drafts started to clear more quickly. She hadn't written a thing like that in almost ten years, even though she'd tried to write the odd paragraph here and there. She'd abandoned the whole practice. But back then, how much had been Sofie's instruction and how much had been Jo's own, bold new writing? As the years slipped past, it became harder to remember, harder to tell who was responsible.

It was true that since getting that email, she'd been thinking about it more and more. She hadn't had the courage to reply, worried that anything she said might be used against her. But she had to admit to herself that it hadn't been the biggest shock. She tried to tease that thought out and understand it, but she couldn't. Shouldn't she be angry? Instead, she was sick with sadness. What did she know of what Sofie had been doing all these years without her? Even though they hadn't spoken since the summer, she thought she'd feel better if she saw Sofie in the flesh. She had mulled this thought over for days, letting herself feel worse and worse. All she had to do was ask Sofie. All she had to do was ask her.

* * *

Jo turned up empty-handed at Sofie's gates that evening. She rang twice before she was buzzed in. When she saw Sofie, she did feel better. Her hair was loose around her shoulders and she seemed more relaxed than when she was putting on a big show with what she was wearing. She was just in a T-shirt. It made her look normal.

Jo had texted Sofie earlier in the day to ask if she could stop over for a drink and had been told there was sloe gin and an empty sofa waiting.

When they walked into the kitchen, Jo could see the bottle was already out, along with two empty glasses. She liked thinking Sofie had been waiting for her. Next to them were several bottles of high-end juice and the Jiffy bag they must have come in. She snorted.

'On a health kick? You always said green juice tasted like grass.'

Sofie shrugged, unperturbed.

'It does, but beauty is pain.' She got out a fresh glass and handed it to Jo, pouring the gin over a handful of ice. Then she refreshed her own glass, leaving one on the side, and took a sip. She smiled, and Jo knew that smile. It was a smile that said: I've won. Jo was used to it. Sofie was always winning.

'What are you looking so pleased about?' Jo took a sip from her gin and set the glass back down. She'd once been immeasurably jealous of things like Sofie's glassware, but now nothing bothered her.

Sofie smiled, her face flushed pink, as though she'd just had a hot bath. 'I'm just happy you're here.'

Jo heard a faint thud from upstairs. It was light enough that it could have been anything falling to the floor, but the look on Sofie's face told her different. Jo could tell she'd been drinking for a while.

'Is there someone here?' Jo looked out at the garden but couldn't see beyond the black glass. No one knew she was here, and the house was secluded from the neighbours. It never used to give her jitters before.

Sofie put her glass down.

'You don't have to look so worried!' She nodded towards the

juice. 'A student popped round with a little delivery and she's just on her way out.'

'Three days before Christmas? Shouldn't they be released from your clutches this late in the year?'

Sofie laughed.

'Apparently not.'

Jo's mouth was sticky and sweet from the gin.

'Does she have a name?'

Sofie sucked on a finger that was damp from her glass.

'Of course. Alice. But I like to call her my little *Schnecke*.'

Jo was unsurprised. She, of course, had been something similar to Sofie once.

'Is this who you were so enamoured with when I came over in the summer?'

Sofie's face dropped briefly.

'No,' she said. 'That was someone I was quite wrong about. He had too much of an ego to take any feedback.'

Yes, Sofie's star student had been a man. But it hadn't taken her long to find a replacement.

'What will you do with her?' said Jo.

'Men are always disappointing, each in their own way, aren't they?' said Sofie. 'I don't know what I was thinking.'

When Alice finally appeared at the kitchen door, waving sheepishly, she was fairly unremarkable. A woman in her early to mid-twenties, she looked flushed and bumbling. Jo introduced herself, and Alice's soft face looked up at her and then at Sofie. She seemed embarrassed but pleased to be in their company.

'Stay for another drink,' said Sofie.

'Oh, no, thank you,' she said. 'I don't want to get in your way.'

Jo was relieved.

The girl seemed bright and hopeful. In her own way, pulling her rucksack carelessly over a shoulder, vulnerable. Jo tried to imagine a great outpouring of words coming from her. She tried to imagine this young woman had a world of thoughts and feelings that were beautifully articulated and valuable, but all she could think was: you haven't lived. Go away and live and write about it later. Get out and live.

After Alice left, Sofie seemed perky and verbose. She was cheerful in a way that bothered Jo, but she didn't let the feeling stick. She knew that with a few words, she could tear Sofie down. She didn't do it straight away. Instead, she watched as Sofie grew more and more animated, throwing some olives in a bowl and impulsively kissing Jo on both cheeks while telling a story from her childhood. It was easy, like watching something get carried away by the tide.

After a couple more drinks, Sofie made a quip about Jo's 'little ad campaigns'. *There.* Jo had been waiting for her moment.

'A few days ago, I got an email from a journalist,' she said.

Four

Alice

It wasn't hard to find her online, but only because she had a fairly unusual name. It was obvious that she'd tried to remove herself from the swell of internet searches that linked her to Sofie.

Jocasta Franklin didn't even have a Wikipedia page. In many ways, she was a ghost. But even internet ghosts have jobs, and those at marketing agencies will have some kind of online footprint. I don't know what I thought I'd do when I found her. I studied her headshot on her company's website and read the two-line bio over and over again. It was apparently common knowledge that Sofie had once been married to a woman, but the details had been hazy. The thing is, she was always a writer first. The finer details about her life seemed immaterial.

I'd been avoiding Walt since our last conversation, leaving early for work and then locking myself in my room to write whenever I was in halls. I thought all the time about his face when he said, *I don't want you to leave me. I want you to help me.* My head raced with everything he'd said about Sofie, and I tried to marry it up with how she always acted with me: polite, generous and steely, as though nothing could touch her. I couldn't imagine her laughing in bed and sharing confidences with one of her male students. I couldn't comprehend why a woman in her glass house would want anything to do with him at all.

But what was the point of making it up?

That day, I could see my breath as I walked through the open greenery to the Students' Union for a coffee. It was the day before Christmas Eve and I wanted to stock up on junk food and drinks on the way. As always, the area was like a wind tunnel, and the force of it pushed me back. It felt good, in a way, and I wondered if the wind would push me all the way back to Cambridge, where my parents were inevitably sitting in the living room circling programmes in the *Radio Times*.

But I was here, fuelled by Americanos and Skittles, with some misguided feeling about getting my work done. Was Sofie working too? I imagined her curled up with Jocasta in her little reading nook in the kitchen, reading poetry to each other and drinking bulbous gin and tonics.

I passed through another building on the way to the Union, which had a shop in the basement full of pale sandwiches and energy drinks. I worked my way through the aisles, pulling off various items without much thought, opening a packet of Hula Hoops and slipping one salty loop onto my tongue, crunching down until it turned to mulch in my mouth. I swallowed in front of the cashier, putting my armful of snacks in front of him. He looked at the open packet of crisps and told me I shouldn't do that.

'But I'm paying for it now,' I said, as he loaded my shopping into a thin plastic bag.

He tutted.

'You could've eaten the whole lot and then decided not to pay.'

I took another handful of crisps out of the packet, crunching loudly, thinking about what he'd said.

'If I wasn't going to pay, I'd just walk out the shop,' I told him. 'I wouldn't eat them in front of you.'

He picked up the open packet between two fingers, holding the scanner up to it as though it was contaminated. When I'd paid, I wished him a Merry Christmas, but he just shook his head.

Walt was waiting for me at the entrance, snapping a red lace between his teeth and holding a bag full of chocolate bars.

'It's you,' I said, though I felt oddly unsurprised to see him. 'I just got told off for opening my crisps before leaving the shop.'

'You didn't actually pay for all of it, did you?'

I tried to work out if he was joking.

He reached into his pocket and took out several extra chocolate bars. 'It's so expensive in there. You know the rule is like, buy one get one free.'

I didn't point out that he could obviously afford the extortionate campus prices.

'Why are you here?'

He took another bite from his lace.

'Here, at the shop?'

'Here, on campus.'

'It's too late to get a flight home. Plus, the whole Christmas thing is sort of meaningless in our house. Can I walk you to the Students' Union for a coffee?'

I nodded and we walked side by side up the stairs and across a courtyard. It almost felt as though nothing had happened. I wondered if he remembered our last conversation, the drunken but delicate way he'd touched my shoulder.

'You seem a little brighter,' I said. 'Better, even.'

He laughed. 'I am, actually.'

He held the door open for me and insisted on paying for my coffee. We sat down at a table and I felt ready to hear an explanation for the things he'd said, to hear what had really happened.

'I've switched tutors,' he said, pressing a finger into his mince pie.

We could choose Robert to coach us through our novels, of course, but if you were lucky enough to get into Sofie's group, you generally stayed there.

'Did you have a falling-out with Sofie about your work?'

He replied slowly and deliberately, as though talking to a child.

'Yes, of course. But only after everything that happened. Only after I gave her back her mug and told her to leave me alone.'

'Really? *You* told *her* to leave *you* alone?'

'I thought you'd get it.' He crumbled a piece of pastry until it turned to dust on his plate. 'I thought of all people, you'd listen.'

'I am listening,' I said. I paused, thinking about how to put my words together in the right way. 'You clearly had some sort of close relationship with her no one knew about, and it's obvious she doesn't have the most . . . orthodox teaching methods.'

Walt snorted. 'Sounds like you've read the same script as the Vice Provost.'

'You've spoken to the Vice Provost about this?'

He nodded. I thought about all the outlandish claims he had made. I could picture Walt going to Sofie for help with his work, and Sofie being overfamiliar, getting too close. But beyond that, my imagination failed me. It all felt so absurd.

He smiled mirthlessly when I didn't react.

'Well, I had to do something.' He reached into his pocket for his phone. 'If you don't believe me, I have evidence. Emails, messages, calls.'

'But that doesn't prove, exactly—'

'What? That she assaulted me? Yes, I suppose nothing will prove that.'

That's the point, I thought. That's the problem.

He turned his phone so I could see the screen, opened a message thread with Sofie's name above it, and started scrolling through. There were reams of messages that he hadn't replied to, and above those a continuous back and forth. But the messages that had been sent to him were longer, paragraphs longer, than what he'd written back. I didn't want to point out that something like this could be faked. How hard would it be to change someone's name to Sofie in your contacts?

What made them compelling was the language. The florid style of communication was so different from her novels, so absurdly so that it was almost more believable. It made sense for Sofie to have another, softer side to her. Her emails to students often rambled extravagantly in a way her prose didn't.

Oh my darling, I can't wait... we'll always have this time together... I miss you wildly, all the time... I'm stroking your face, your twinkling eyes looking up at me... It's what Hardy called the freakishness of love... your soft mouth, the feel of your arms around me...

I stared at it, catching one sentence after the other as he continued to scroll.

'I can hardly believe it,' I said. 'It's hard not to, in a way, but I just can't believe it. She seems so sensible, so together, so intellectual.'

Walt said, 'It's true, she is, but more importantly, she's mercenary. And whatever you once believed about her, you should know that. She's mercenary, greedy. Everyone thinks they're jealous of *her*, but I've never known anyone with such a bottomless pit of covetousness.'

I shook my head.

He said: 'You don't believe me, because in your head she's really something. She's an intellectual titan. But we're so easily blinded from the truth because she's so captivating. She makes it all look so glamorous.'

I thought of her silks snagging against my fingers. The perfectly cut jacket fitting snugly against my waist.

'She is glamorous,' I said.

He looked at me with a worried expression.

'Where did you get that necklace?'

He pointed at my clavicle and I put my hand over it without thinking. Before Jocasta had arrived, Sofie had put together a bag of clothes for me. That night, I'd laid out each item on my bed as though preparing to dress a host of imaginary people. Each piece was unlike anything I'd ever owned or seen, satin shirts and tailored trousers and the most delicate gold locket. It was the first time in my life

I understood why anyone would bother buying expensive things that took up space in their house. I had fondled a particular pair of silk palazzo pants, the style Sofie often wore, and reasoned that if I wore them, eventually my life was bound to catch up, turning me into the kind of person who would wear them. They weren't just things, they were a way of being. And one I wanted, desperately, to materialise.

'It was my mother's,' I lied, opening and closing the locket's clasp with a click.

Walt seemed to believe me.

'She bought me clothes, you know. Nothing so different from what I usually wear.'

That was his way of saying he already had the money to buy nice clothes, and I didn't. Why would I notice an extra cashmere jumper on him? But a gold locket on me stood out like a warning sign. I took my hand away from it.

'I know you don't want to help me,' he said. 'But, Alice, please. Don't be such a disappointment. You have to believe me. At least a little.'

I wondered how his writing was going, whether he felt panicked now the first part of the course was done.

'I met her ex-wife,' I told him. 'It seemed as though they've remained quite close. Maybe she already has a romantic entanglement.'

He pushed his plate away across the table. 'I'm not sure Sofie puts a limit on this stuff.'

'But why would she be pursuing one of her students?'

He shook his head. 'You really don't get it, do you? Her ex-wife is what makes my story credible.'

'Your story,' I said, flatly.

He stood. 'Who do you think gave Sofie that fucking boob mug in the first place? Jo was her star student. Sofie has form. She's done this before.'

I felt sorry for him. It was a pleasurable kind of pity, because I was on the outside looking in. I could take some kind of joy in it because if I felt sorry for him, I wouldn't feel that other, heartsick thing. If I thought he was a liar, it was easier to let him go.

'She trusts you,' he said. 'Maybe you could get her to admit to it. Maybe you could do that.' His eyes were on my locket again. 'I thought if I came here, I could escape my real life. I thought I could do something that really mattered to me. Now I might never be able to do it. I'll have to go home and start again.'

I shook my head, staring at his plateful of crumbs. 'If you want to do it, you'll find a way.'

He looked resigned. 'There is no other way. There's only Sofie's way.'

'I don't know *how* to help you,' I said. 'I only came here to write.'

'You can be extremely cold, Alice,' he said. 'Do you know that? You can be sweet and interesting, and sometimes stupefyingly beautiful. But you can be cold, too.'

I opened my mouth, searching for something to say, and then closed it again.

'You don't believe me now,' he said, 'but you will.' His face was hard and composed. 'And it'll be too late. I promise you that.'

Posted by martin_aimle55

Has anyone else been harassed by Sofie Muller?

I debated whether or not I should post this, but I've spent months dealing with this situation on my own and now wonder if this has happened to other people.

My writing tutor, Sofie Muller, has been sexually harassing me for a while now. She demands physical affection in return for writing help and often calls and messages me as though we're in a relationship. I've never given her any indication this is the case, but it's been really hard to set boundaries and tell her where the line is.

One evening, she even invited me over for wine and invited me to go to bed with her. I was horrified and left immediately, but she emailed me the next day to say how much she cared about me and couldn't bear it when we're apart.

There are stories online that she can be manipulative and controlling and often has a favourite student. I'm now wondering whether this is what people meant by 'favourite.'

Has this ever happened to anyone else? Any stories would be welcome.

25 comments

Five

Jo

'What?' Sofie said. She seemed to have frozen, her drink held up in mid-air, as though someone had pressed 'pause' on her life.

Jo repeated her killer blow: 'I got an email from a journalist.' She regretted the casual way she'd said it now.

Sofie lowered her drink and looked at her. She was known for her silences, and was an expert at deploying them to keep the other person talking.

Succumbing to the silence, Jo said, 'I didn't know how to tell you. It happened a few days ago . . .' She tailed off, unsure how to proceed. Even without speaking, it felt like Sofie was telling her off.

After a beat, Sofie seemed to realise her mistake. Jo was the one with the information, and it had to be coaxed out of her. She smiled.

'It's okay, darling. You can tell me all about it.' Sofie held out a hand from across the sofa.

It felt natural to comply. Jo rearranged herself so her back was against the sofa's arm. 'Maybe we don't need to talk about this now,' she said, crossing her legs.

Sofie was sitting next to her, an inch too close.

Jo cleared her throat.

'It was an investigative journalist. She sent a couple of emails. She's from a big newspaper, I can't remember which one,' she lied.

Sofie was watching her intently, her eyes searching Jo's face.

'She said she's gathering evidence from former students that you . . .' Jo knew as soon as she said the words that Sofie would have to respond, somehow. Was it real?

Sofie waited, unmoving.

'That you plagiarised their work.'

Sofie blinked, absorbing it seemingly without feeling. A second later, she laughed. 'Oh! Well, what a relief,' she said, tossing her hair off her shoulder.

'It is?'

'Of course. May I see the emails?'

Jo had already thought about that.

'I deleted them straight away.'

'Right.' Sofie moved further into the kitchen, as though that was the end of that.

Jo got up to follow her, standing by the bookcase in front of the sofa. She was relieved by Sofie's confidence.

'Don't you wonder who the students are?'

Sofie was pouring herself another sloe gin, filling her tumbler almost to the top.

'Do I wonder?' she mused aloud. She took a sip, looking out towards the garden. 'No, I don't. Everyone wants their little story, don't they? No doubt they think it'll help their careers. They don't realise how juvenile it is.' Sofie raised her voice by an octave. '*I wrote a story about the weather and then she wrote a story about the weather.* Please. They've got nothing to back this up.'

Jo couldn't help but laugh at that. 'It's true, I suppose nothing is original.'

'Nothing,' Sofie said distractedly. 'That doesn't mean this won't be bad though.'

Jo had already considered it. The headlines they'd print, the stuff they'd share on social media. Every time you googled Sofie's name. Even Jo's name, if they mentioned her. It was a big paper, the kind of place that had traction. The kind of place that tried not to make unfounded claims.

Jo could feel in Sofie's silence that she was thinking all this too.

Sofie let out a frustrated sound.

'And to think I had to read all their shitty little stories. For years. Do you remember how much shit I had to read?'

'Of course I do. I was there, remember, I read them too.'

They used to talk about the work all the time. Sofie would hand her the printed pages in bed and they'd laugh at things together. An awkward turn of phrase, a whole plot point that was derivative, the grandiose way the students wrote about their own novels. *This scene will appear in the first section, before you know that John is the killer, but after you realise that something strange is going on. It will be a huge shock to the readers once they know the truth.* That kind of thing, all the time. It was all so vulnerable and oozing, which made it pitiful.

Jo used to think writing fiction was brave before she saw how Sofie read. Every time she wrote, she could see Sofie pointing at a sentence and laughing. *That would never happen,* she could imagine her saying. *That doesn't even make sense. That's so onanistic, so saccharine, so facile.* It was enough to put her off the written word altogether, until she had her little idea.

It was Jo's idea originally, wasn't it? She'd thought about it for months and held it in her mind as though it was the most delicious secret. Really, it was nothing. Just the kernel of a concept, about a woman fascinated by a bird. But it had lodged itself there and she knew there was only one way it was getting out.

She looked up and realised she was holding one of Sofie's novels in her hand. The one with a bird on the cover. She hadn't meant to pick it up, but it was like a reflex. She wanted to squeeze the weight of it between her fingers.

Sofie noticed and came over to her, her face pained and humourless.

'I didn't mean you,' Sofie said, her tone gentle now, soft like a marshmallow. 'You know I didn't mean you.'

'I know.' Jo wondered whether to put the book down or whether that would just draw attention to it. Instead, she held it away from her body awkwardly, as though it had nothing to do with her.

'All this for a few pages stuck together with glue,' Sofie took the book from her, her long nails squeezing into the cover. She held the paperback until she'd indented it with faint crescent moons. 'I always told you, didn't I? How good you were?'

'You did.'

'You know you were my creative lighthouse. And it's obvious now, isn't it? What have I written of any significance since you've been gone?'

This was the kind of feeling that Jo tried to forget. The way Sofie made her feel powerful. Jo was the one with the light; she had talent, ideas, dedication. She was the lighthouse, whirling around on the spot, guiding Sofie to safety. Without her, Sofie was adrift. Without her, she was nothing.

'And with your first novel,' Sofie said. 'It even won a prize and I never said I had anything to do with it.'

Sofie was right. All this trouble for a few pieces of paper stuck together with glue. But then, everything boiled down to its component parts sounded redundant. What was the human heart but a few valves and some blood? Jo looked up and realised Sofie was waiting to find out what Jo would do next. For a moment, Jo had all the power, and it felt good. She could get drunk on watching Sofie try to anticipate her next move. The dynamic between them occasionally used to switch like this. Most days Sofie had control. But the rare times when Jo had the upper hand, it almost made Sofie seem fragile, which gave Jo the idea that their relationship was tolerable.

She thought if Sofie begged, if she got down on her knees and begged in this moment, she could do it again. She could be both lighthouse and storm for her. But hadn't she always said that to her in moments of weakness? In just a beat or two the whole thing would curdle and Jo would be on the back foot again, pleading, desperate for praise.

She logged the feeling away to take out and examine later. Sofie had said she was a good writer. She'd said it, once.

Sofie took a step towards her. Somehow, when Jo looked down, the novel had ended up on the floor.

'You *didn't* delete the emails, did you?'

Jo swallowed.

'I don't want you to read them.'

Sofie was looking right at her. It was like sitting in the sun on a Friday afternoon, when the whole world is drunk on its own possibility. Sofie was touching her forearm, fondling the spot where she had once told her the freckles looked like Orion's Belt. Perfectly positioned and easy to spot. She used to kiss them: one, two, three.

'I'm sorry, Jocasta.'

The grip on her arm tightened painfully. Jo smiled, like it was a joke. Sofie used to smack her sometimes, lightly, in the moment, and would then relish the way Jo's body arched upwards in pleasure. Sofie had a way of doing things without being asked. She took enjoyment in guessing correctly.

'I'm sorry you have to deal with these emails. It has nothing to do with you.' She loosened her grip and slid her hand up Jo's arm, touching the top of her shoulder.

'Even if it doesn't, it does, because I used to be your wife.' It still thrilled Jo to say the word, and it made Sofie smile.

'People used to laugh about it. That my wife left me.' Her mouth was travelling across Jo's shoulder now, as though it was inspecting a foreign object. She released her tongue as it slid down the length of her arm towards her elbow and then one, two, three kisses on her freckles.

'They can't have laughed. I don't think they laughed.' Jo let her arm be held. It was warm and comforting, and she would gladly take Sofie's apology. She'd dated other women in the years since, but none like Sofie. Didn't everyone want to be touched like they were an object of fascination?

Jo had tried to stay away from her, but the email had brought her back again. She couldn't help it. She was angry and confused, but falling for Sofie was as natural as falling asleep.

Sofie looked up at her.

'I promise you they did.' Sofie lowered herself to the floor until she was on her knees. She held up her hands as though in supplication and Jo took them, sliding down beside her.

'It wasn't ever funny,' said Jo.

Sofie put a hand under Jo's top. Jo didn't stop her although she did take a sharp breath, drawing her belly in like a reflex.

'I used to touch you like this all the time and there was never anything strange about it,' said Sofie. Her hand was resting on Jo's ribcage, spread around the curve of bones. 'Now if I want to, I have to get on my knees. I have to ask you for permission.'

'No, you don't need to do that.'

Sofie took this as an acquiescence and moved her fingers to the curve of Jo's breast, squeezing the soft flesh upwards. Jo let out a breath and then kissed Sofie's mouth. It was familiar and exciting, the small bite down on Jo's lower lip, the feel of Sofie's hot breath on her cheek. She knew this whole routine by heart, which made it no less thrilling. Sofie only wanted to see Jo gasp in delight, it was as though she fed on it. That was the pull for her: the ecstasy of others.

Jo craved being the object of her affection, even so many years later. It made her feel needed and wanted, and there was nothing like the right person touching you at the wrong time. It was illicit and strange and fed the urge for sexual shock that Jo often found herself wanting. Sometimes, she would walk down the street and wonder what would happen if she put her hand through that woman's hair in front of her, what it would feel like to thread a finger through the loop of a stranger's jeans.

Sofie was murmuring in her ear.

'I am nothing without you. There is no beauty in my life, no affection – no writing. I want to make you come. You know no one can do it quite like me. I'll take you right to the point you like and then draw back, and then we'll go again.'

This kind of talk always worked because Jo liked to think of herself as something Sofie would enjoy toying with, just for the fun of it. Sofie was sliding off Jo's jeans, pulling at her underwear, when Jo's leg hit against the book on the floor. It had a bird on the cover. The bird looked melancholy, and not in the way it was supposed to. Had it really always looked like that?

'Tell me again. Tell me I'm a good writer,' she said. The feeling of Sofie between her legs made her whole body feel safe. She could imagine walking through a world that was quiet and untouched and made of snow.

'You are, you are, I'll tell you as many times as you want me to,' said Sofie. 'I only want you to be happy, everything I have done was in search of your happiness.'

Jo laid out her body for Sofie, spread her legs wider, delighted by Sofie's delight in her. She felt that she would give her everything in that moment, more than she'd ever given. She'd do anything she wanted. She'd give her her body, her time, her words. She felt the hard edge of the book underneath the palm of her hand as she cried out unexpectedly. The feeling took her by surprise. She knew when this moment was over, she might feel differently.

Until then, she'd do anything, anything, anything.

The next day, Jo received another email. It began with an apology for the abruptness of the first two messages, but the journalist wanted her to understand that the story would be going to print this year, with or without her input. There would be a claim that one of the short pieces Jo wrote on the creative writing course she attended almost two decades earlier bore a striking resemblance to parts of Sofie's most popular work. Could Jo verify or deny that this was the case?

The particular claim was being brought forward by another student who had studied in the same year as Jo, who would remain anonymous. The journalist had copies of the story that had been passed around the class and marked up as they read. The student remembered, in particular detail, how Sofie had been taken with the story. It was shortly after that it was claimed Jo had entered into a romantic relationship with Sofie, while she was still her student. Could this, also, be confirmed or denied?

Their civil partnership in the early noughties, the email continued, was a matter of public record. As was the dissolution of the partnership only a few years later. Could Jo speak to what had happened? And did the 1999 novel by Sofie Muller, *A Bird Came Down*, which featured almost verbatim paragraphs from the story that Jo had allegedly written, receive any input from Jo? It was noted, indeed, that she is mentioned in the acknowledgements as Sofie's 'muse, provocateur and left-hand woman'. It was also noted that a similar acknowledgement was made of Sofie in Jo's first and only novel. Could Jo comment on whether it was simply a fruitful creative partnership, or – in light of claims made by other students that their ideas, words, and in some instances, entire plot lines and paragraphs, had made it into Sofie's novels – was there something more coercive at play?

The sender would be much obliged to receive Jo's response to the above matters by return.

Jo was at her desk at work when she read it, and closed her browser with a click. The agency was quiet after the Christmas break, and she was meant to be trawling through pages of website copy for a logistics company based in mainland Europe. The company was opening a new distribution centre that would be over one million square feet. It was a colossal thing that had been haunting her. She was meant to be injecting voice and character into the pages that explained how the company sourced, built and helped to outfit these spaces for investors and occupiers. That day, she was writing the copy for its sustainability page, trying to find a new way to say 'ethical social governance' for the tenth time. She'd made a joke earlier to one of her colleagues about how her experience writing fiction came in handy with clients like this, but the joke had fallen flat.

Later that day, she would be presenting the first few pages to the client on a video call. She was going to explain that the tone of voice she'd chosen was confident, but conversational. It also had to work across thirty different translations, so she'd had to scrub out any idioms or colloquial English. This was easier said than done when trying to find a fun way to talk about spaces so large that they enveloped her mind.

She mentioned to the colleague sitting next to her that her first flat had been 500 square feet, and she'd thought that was big. 'A million,' she repeated, 'a *million* square feet. It's the kind of thing that belongs on Mars.'

Her colleague turned away from his three screens of Photoshop to entertain her tangent. He shrugged. 'When people buy all that crap on the internet, and it comes the next day, where do they think it comes from?'

She wanted to say the number one million had made her feel bad. She hadn't felt bad about writing copy for people who owned warehouses before, but that number had brought it home to her. It was nothing to them, and they had dozens of spaces across Europe like it. Spaces like that were the new world order, and in her own small way, it was how she in turn made her living. Instead, she asked if he bought things online for next-day delivery.

Her colleague had turned back to his screens. He clicked an image of a woman's headshot and it changed to black-and-white. 'Of course,' he said. 'But I don't feel good about it.' He inclined his head towards the novel that sat on her desk next to her sandwich. 'We can't all be creatives and starving artists, can we? We've all got to make a living.' He did a double take at the book and said he recognised it from years ago. Didn't it once win a big prize?

'Yes,' Jo said, laying her hand across the cover. 'It actually won several, though of course people only remember the biggest.'

He picked it up and thumbed across its edges, as though it was a deck of playing cards.

'You've turned down quite a few corners,' he pointed out.

'I'm looking for a particular passage. I've already read it several times.'

He grunted. 'A lot of things don't merit re-reading. Some things don't even merit reading once.'

'That's true, but this book is special to me. I knew the author back when it came out, almost twenty years ago.'

He read out the title. '*A Bird Came Down*. What kind of bird is that on the cover?'

'It's a species native to the Himalayas,' she said. 'The book is about a woman who's obsessed with finding this bird, but the only way she can get out to India to look for it is to accept an invitation from a friend to stay in the Himalayan mountains. The friend is a travel writer who has sailed around Cape Horn and lived with nomads, but none of that matters to the woman because she just wants to find the bird.'

'So, what happens to her?'

That seemed like a simple question, but it wasn't. It went like this: Sofie wanted the book to be a murder mystery; the woman had got up early to birdwatch on her own and had spotted some illegal business, putting her life at risk. But Jo had to explain that the story wasn't about death. It was about love. The woman loved the bird, and she loved the process of hunting for the bird. The whole story was really about not only her desire to be alone but also the necessity of being alone in order to be quiet and invisible enough to see the thing she'd been looking for all these years. It was about the gap of understanding her friend's life fell into. It was about the unspoken jealousy between the woman and her friend the travel writer, who went from country to country trying to find an answer to some unanswerable question, while her friend was satisfied by one simple, small thing.

She decided this was too much to explain. 'The woman ends up murdered and the travel writer has to decide whether to avenge it or cover it up,' she said.

'Huh. You know, it sounds pretty good. I love a crime novel.'

'It was originally supposed to be genre-bending fiction, or something like that.'

He looked at her. 'So you think it should've ended differently?' He put the book back reverentially beside her mouse. 'It's hard when a character you like ends up dying.'

'It was devastating. The ending left me devastated.'

'Well, I guess when you write a novel, you can end it however you like.'

Jo smiled, agreed and went back to her pages of copy.

Sofie had won the argument. All plots started to sound idiotic when you said them out loud, and Sofie knew it. So she made Jo explain it to her, again and again, watching her without saying anything. Even when Jo had finished talking about where she thought the narrative should go, Sofie remained silent. The silence that could fill a room. She won every argument like that, by just looking at her, by explaining with her eyes that Jo's thoughts were occasionally bright, but mostly stupid. There was so much that fell into that silence. The silence could tear down buildings and fill up concert halls, it could turn editors and agents from people with stature into bumbling fools. It could climb the height of skyscrapers and come back down, intact and unceasing.

'Okay,' Jo had said, eventually. 'Maybe you're right. Maybe it does need something to keep it interesting.'

Sofie smiled and the sun fell on Jo again.

'Maybe, actually,' Jo had continued, keen not to lose this feeling, 'it would just be better if you plotted it. That would be better, wouldn't it?'

Had it really been like that? Unending silence until everything made sense again. Jo had got a kiss on the head and a tickle at the nape of her neck for that one. Sofie picked up the pages she'd written in class, years earlier, and reformulated the idea. Then she gave the idea back to Jo, to finish. But the idea was Sofie's now. It made more sense, from a marketing perspective, too, for it to come from Sofie.

She had reassured Jo, 'You'll find something else to write about in your own name, something literary and wonderful. And I'll help you get it published. I'll make damn sure it's published.'

Jo had been giddy with relief that the silence was done and out of the way and they could go back to loving each other.

'Just please don't change the title,' she had said, pitifully. She had felt unsure about relinquishing the book until the announcement of the novel in the trade paper. It was obvious, then, that it would be bigger than anything she could've done on her own. She had helped to boost Sofie's entire career. By then, Jo had a first draft of her own novel, too, and Sofie had helped to shape it.

Could Jo confirm or deny? Confirm or corroborate?

She remembered the argument they'd had after Sofie won the prize and Jo tried to say it was unfair. Did Jo realise it was her fault, she'd made Sofie feel bad?

'It was all lovely before you said that,' Sofie had wept. 'It was a perfect novel and it won a perfect prize and you've ruined it. You've done this, don't you get it? You've taken my greatest achievement away from me. You. Only you. Just you. You made me feel like this.'

But then – Sofie forgave her. They spent the money on stupid things. They were building a life together. It was a relief, to see how much fun Sofie was having. And wasn't it fun? Who wouldn't want all the trappings of success, without the burden of fame? Wasn't that why, when Sofie asked her if she wanted to do it again, she said *yes*, without hesitating?

'Do you have any more ideas?' Sofie had said. 'It doesn't matter if you don't, there are plenty already out there. The writing is the hard part.'

'Out where?' Jo had asked.

Jo's colleague tapped her on the shoulder. 'You're right, I've googled it.'

She blinked into the blue light of her computer screen. 'What?'

'A million square feet. It's the size of sixteen football fields. It's incomprehensible. How did the world get like this?'

'I have no idea,' Jo said, and she meant it.

Six

Alice

In the new year the juice kitchen was busier than I'd ever seen it. Three- and five-day cleanses were rushing out the door and I was asked to work extra shifts to cover the demand. The women making the juice were working eighteen hours at a time and Olena would text to tell me how exhausted she was. I told Molly I was worried about them, but she reassured me it was just a phase. Some of the women had other jobs as the hours at the juice kitchen weren't normally reliable. Often, they would leave after twelve hours, go clean houses and then return to the kitchen to fulfil the rest of the orders.

We weren't allowed meat or dairy in the kitchen as it contravened our vegan manufacturing credentials, so we hid milk in the back of one of the industrial fridges in plastic bags. Every afternoon when I arrived, I would make coffee and Olena would top each cup up with milk. I told the women they had to take a break and sit down, but they shook their heads. The quicker they could get the juice made, the sooner they could go home.

One day in early January, we had just finished our coffees and I'd washed out the mugs before pulling up the orders spreadsheet. Molly had recently got in contact with several actors from a popular reality

TV show set in London, and I was copied into the emails where she offered them free juice in exchange for online content and branding at events. *Darlings!* each email would begin, *How many bottles can we provide you with? To the usual address? You can mix the spicy ginger lemonade with vodka!*

Some of them included lengthy paragraphs about how they must have dinner and not just chat when they run into each other at spinning classes. Sometimes Molly even sent me her Net-à-Porter returns slips and packages to take to the post office. It gave me a glimpse into what she was doing when she wasn't at the kitchen: lunch dates and luxury exercise classes, health events, and co-branding opportunities at art fairs and fashion shows.

Olena laughed when I showed her the emails, then asked if I knew who all these people were.

'Some of them,' I said.

'But you're supposed to be writing,' she told me, 'not looking at people on TV drinking juice.'

'I *am* writing!' I said. 'And they don't actually drink the juice on TV. My tutor is helping me get my novel together and has promised to do what she can to make sure it gets published at the end of the course.'

Olena raised her eyebrows.

'Why can't your parents give you money? Then you wouldn't have to work with all these old women and could just write all day.'

'They don't have extra money to give me.'

She looked unconvinced and pointed to my locket.

'Maybe they just give you money for the wrong things.'

I scrolled through the orders spreadsheet for that day, scanning the list of names.

'Well, I like working. If I just sat in front of my laptop all day, there'd be nothing to write about.'

I spotted Sofie's name on the list, which had become a regular occurrence. I wasn't sure whether she kept ordering the juices because she liked them or because she pitied my little side job. I went to find her order email in the shared inbox and came across an extra note she'd added along with it.

I hate to say it, she wrote, *but last week, there was a hair in my juice. I took a picture (attached), and I'm sure it was a mistake. But just a warning to be careful, sweet juice-makers of the Kingdom of East Angles!*

Underneath was a reply from Molly apologising profusely, saying she was a sweetheart for pointing out the mistake. She would check every juice made with extra care from now on and make sure it'd never happen again. The next round of juices would, of course, be on her.

My stomach twisted as I read it.

'What's wrong?' Olena asked.

I showed her the email and she started shaking her head.

'No, I don't believe it. That would never happen.' She pointed at the hairnet she was wearing.

'I know.'

I clicked out of the email chain and told her it wasn't a reflection on her work.

She scowled.

'They do this to get free juice.'

'You think so? Why would someone with money do that? Maybe it was just a harmless mistake,' I said.

'No, they do it because they spend a lot of money, and they want something for free. This isn't good. Sometimes I walk through the kitchen when my shift is done and forget to put the hairnet back on. If Molly sees me, I get lectured for hours.' Her eyes started to well up.

I closed my laptop and got up. 'Oh, no, please don't cry. I'm sure you're right, she might have just made it up to see what we would do.'

'But this lady is your friend, isn't she? Why would she do this?' A small tear escaped and ran down her pink cheek.

'I'm sure it was just a mistake, it could've happened anywhere, to anyone.' I patted her arm. 'Don't cry,' I said again. 'It isn't worth crying about.'

'It's a bad omen,' Olena said, wiping at her face. 'I knew it, I knew it.'

'You knew what?'

'I finally told my husband about what I found, and that I was going to leave him.'

'Really? Oh. That's so brave of you. That's so brave.'

She looped a finger under her hairnet and readjusted it, looking out towards the kitchen. 'He said I'd ruined everything by saying this, and that he knew I'd been seeing another man. That we couldn't pretend any more and I would have to leave. That I'd get nothing and my family would be so ashamed when they found out. Everyone would know about me and my life would be ruined.' She put her hands up to her face and sobbed. 'It's all my fault. He's right. I've ruined my own life.'

'No, no, no,' I assured her. 'You haven't. No, no.'

'You said it would be better to be honest, but I knew even then you were wrong. Sometimes it's better to lie. It's just better and easier to lie.'

She pulled away from me.

'I am so sorry,' I said. 'I only wanted you to be happy and free. I only wanted you to live the life you wanted without being beholden to anyone.'

'Like you?'

I opened my mouth to answer but she sniffed and threw back her head.

'The people who waste their money on these things, they deserve to find a hair to choke them in the back of the throat.' She jabbed a finger at her chest. 'I'm the best at my job. I work hard, and I'm the best at it.'

'Yes! You are.'

'Well, they can have their little fun and try and get me in trouble.

And they can drink their juice now that they've made their little complaint. But next time they drink it, they'll have to wonder.' She threw her hands up and stormed towards the fridge, pulling out litre bottles. 'They'll have to think about if it tastes good because of apples and spinach or because I spit in it,' she said.

In the spring term, our classes took on a new level of urgency. The novels were coming together in earnest. We workshopped our plots, pulled at each other's threads and ignored well-meaning advice – we would just write what we wanted to write. I compiled thousands of words on my protagonist, who was trapped in a loveless marriage. I toyed with what she desired and what she'd do: abandon her marriage, or embrace her role as mistress? Go mad and murder her husband, or resign herself to a life of quiet misery? I spent so much time thinking about what she wanted and who she was that when I went to the juice kitchen, it was almost as if I was living in a dream that I had created. I snatched jokes from strangers on buses, I used the names of my childhood friends, and I wanted to steal other students' opening sentences. I was a parasite engorged by other people's lives, and there was no limit to what I would take.

Some of the students chose to write their novel with Robert rather than Sofie, which surprised me, and Walt now only turned up to the classes that Sofie wasn't teaching. He no longer had anything to do with her and his absence became so normal that I wanted to ask Sofie if she remembered who he was. For the most part, I tried not to think about him, or think about him thinking about me. The less I saw him, the easier it became.

Sofie continued to push me, in and out of class. I attended more tutorials at her house, where she would pull out pages of notes she'd made about my writing and where it could be improved. She drilled me for more plot points and urged me to go further. She'd pick apart the structure of my work and the language I chose and told me what I'd just about got away with.

She teased apart my writing tics: adverbs, clichés, point of view slips and mixed metaphors. She struck out in pen the muffled ways I tried to express myself: *It's almost as if.* I needed more specificity, she told me, to pull off the whole trick. Universal stories are told through unique experiences.

I absorbed it all, feeling myself pulled towards the kind of writing I never thought I'd be able to accomplish. But without Sofie's unfaltering belief in what I could achieve, I doubt much of what my multiple notebooks contained would have held any value. There was magic in being edited, chiselling away through her tireless assessment. The constant redrafting brought the work into clearer focus, but the process became more and more subconscious. I would read the lines back and wonder when I wrote them. Had I been there? Where did that plot point emerge from? It was all inextricably linked to Sofie.

And so, as the season shifted towards spring and my novel started to take shape, I found myself spending more and more time with her. A couple of times, she emailed me on my personal email and I switched back to my university address as though it had been a mistake. She called me on my mobile, asking if I could still make our tutorials. She sent messages to me recommending TV shows and films she watched that had similar themes to my novel. She emailed me paragraphs of her opinions of titles I'd recommended. She signed off each note with: *S xx* and I replied with a disinterested: *Thanks!*

How many hours had she and Walt spent messaging and emailing? How much did he probe her for advice and encouragement? I felt her attention shift towards me, and imagined how far her communication would go if I didn't periodically withdraw. It was unsettling, to think about what Walt had said about her now that I seemed to have ignited her curiosity.

There were several nights when I thought about walking to his halls and knocking on his door. Sometimes, I saw him walking across campus and my heart would thud and flutter like a church bell. I longed for everything to go back to normal, but it was somehow easier not to acknowledge him. Weeks passed like this, the idea of him and his story passing into obscurity. That was, until he reappeared in real life.

Henderson was getting a divorce. He told us in the pub in town after class one evening, squinting down at his beer. After a few minutes, I realised this was because he was trying to stop himself from crying. I couldn't imagine what he was feeling so I just sat quietly as he told us what she'd said to him, how they didn't do enough together any more, the gigantic distance that had opened up. He shook his head.

'I was constantly asking her to do things with me and she always said no. I couldn't win.'

Now, he had shared custody of their almost teenaged son. He started bringing him to the occasional evening class when he couldn't find a babysitter. The boy would sit in the back and listen to music on his phone or read a paperback, while Sofie talked and we workshopped each other's novels. He was skinny and tall, his shoulders hunched over as though he was afraid of how much vertical space he took up in the world.

I expected Sofie to be disturbed by a tween presence in her classes, but she seemed unaffected, addressing him as 'Young Stuart'. Sometimes, she walked past and gave him an extra handout in case he was interested, smiling with mischief. I felt relieved when I saw Henderson, once her most loathed student, smile back at her.

During our fifteen-minute break during class one evening, Henderson and I went and got coffee and chocolate from the Union, while Young Stuart stayed at the back of class, occupied with his phone.

Henderson said writing was harder now his mind was so occupied with grief. 'I know it's a terrible thing to say,' he said, flicking his plastic coffee lid, 'But it's as though the woman I married has died. I don't recognise her at all.'

'It must be so difficult,' I told him, and looked at him hard, thinking about the marriage in my novel. When Henderson was younger, he might have had presence. I could picture him tall and gregarious. Now, he was hunched over, drinking his coffee like he was offering an apology. The contrast made me feel deeply sorry for him.

'I feel terrible for Stuart,' he said, a catch in his voice. I interjected as though I hadn't noticed, said Young Stuart seemed like a patient and diligent boy.

Henderson nodded. 'I thought about dropping out. I didn't think I'd be able to finish the course now I have to look after him every other week. But Sofie insisted I bring him along.'

This surprised me.

'Sofie did?'

'She said that nothing should stop me writing and what did it matter if he sat in the back of the classroom. She's sweet with him.'

I raised my eyebrows.

'So, you've found her soft spot then.'

Henderson laughed.

'Maybe. Maybe she just felt sorry for me.'

'Or maybe she didn't want a good writer to go to waste.'

His face turned serious and he pushed his glasses up his nose.

'I wanted to ask you something.' His eyes darted to the wide glass doors that led out to the pavement where the rest of the class was smoking and milling about.

'Sure,' I said. 'You can ask me anything.'

'Last term, when you asked if I thought Sofie ever slept with her students, was that because of Walt?'

My eyes searched his face.

'Why, what did he tell you?'

He sighed.

'That she assaulted him. I couldn't believe it, you know. She was always so aloof and severe with us. And now that I've found myself in a difficult situation, she's been nothing but kind.' He grimaced. 'Why would she do that?'

'He's been trying to convince me of the whole thing for weeks, but it never made any sense,' I said. 'I felt guilty about it, just because, what if it was true? And I'd told him to piss off.'

'I thought he might have told you and I wanted you to know.' He leaned forward, his elbow knocking his chocolate bar. I saved it from falling off the table, but he didn't notice. 'He showed me these text messages from her, loads of them. So, I asked to look myself and took the phone. I clicked into the contact he'd named 'Sofie' and memorised the number. When I went home and compared it to the one she gave us, it was completely different.'

'Really?' I swallowed. It felt good, to hear what I wanted to hear.

'The next time I saw him I told him he was young and stupid, and this whole thing wasn't going to do him any favours. He was so shocked that his whole face went red, and he just didn't have anything to say.'

'You think he sent them to himself from a different phone?' I asked. 'You think he made them up?'

Henderson shrugged, nodding. 'It's crazy, isn't it. What he's trying to spread about her is crazy. I mean, do you really think Sofie is some mastermind sitting at home texting her students from a burner phone? What kind of person has two phones?'

I looked down at my coffee cup and felt the liquid cooling down inside it. I brought the cup to my lips and felt the bitter tang wash over my teeth.

'Right,' I said. 'What kind of person.'

'You have to be careful, Alice,' he said. 'I know you two were close.'

'Oh, I am, I am being careful.'

'You still care about him, I can tell. But these situations . . . they're better left alone.'

I looked at him without saying anything.

'You have to look out for yourself,' he said. 'That's what everyone else is doing.'

It was nice to be told this. It made me think that Walt would've been upset to be chastised by Henderson, always so calm and steady.

'What if we're wrong though?'

'We're not.'

When we went back to class, I looked at Sofie's face as she flicked through pages of our work. She caught my eye and smiled, as though something warm had been on her mind.

Seven

It rained all the time. The smell of it by the lake reminded me of my childhood, and sometimes I breathed in my heavy, sodden clothes when I got back to my room. I had a new practice of writing things down in my diary that were important to me: I was trying to teach myself to be grateful, while at the same time allowing myself to cheat on my novel. Sofie said this was important.

The aroma of old books, the grumble dogs make in their sleep, like a kettle boiling. Those sticky, sweet pies from the deli in town. The salt crust left on everything from the sea air.

Sometimes I sat at my desk in a coat Sofie had given me, a cashmere blend. I stroked its arm and pretended for a brief moment I would grow up to be someone like her. I knew I'd be too embarrassed to ever go and visit my parents wearing this coat. The questions that would follow would have no logical answers. But it felt good to wrap it around me and feel like a character in a Doris Day film, perhaps with a matching hat and gloves. I was beautiful and whimsical and of course everything I wrote would arrive naturally onto the page. It would be witty and self-possessed and effortless. The kind of person who wore this coat would be completely without challenges. Just like the soft wool that people wanted to reach out and touch, everything around her was wrapped in a fuzzy haze, like in a dream. The good kind of dream.

It was easy for me to imagine things like this when I shut my dorm room door and listened to the pattering of the rain on the window. I would drink a small beetroot juice and a cup of tea with custard creams, and I would be satiated by my own work for hours.

But every so often when I was writing my lists, I would find myself feeling grateful for stupid things, like Walt's face. It was hard to let go of a face like that, one I'd warmed to so quickly. I would bare my teeth and audibly gurgle, a strange ritual to try and replace the thought with sound. I reminded myself to focus on the writing, only worry about the writing. This was Sofie's mantra: keep writing.

Even though our time at university was set up to accommodate this way of life, there was so much that bled over the edges of our work. I was constantly worrying about the juice kitchen and Olena; I thought of my parents and tried to be diligent about calling them. Sometimes, I thought about my ex-boyfriend and the way he'd move his tongue over the lace of my bra before pulling it off. It was hard to write around these things, so inevitably they worked themselves onto the page. I could feel myself leaking, and the more I wrote, the harder it was to contain every thought or feeling I'd ever had, like I was carrying them around in an open cardboard box everywhere I went.

As the Easter holidays neared, the weather started to improve. I had a tutorial booked with Sofie to workshop my latest chapters and she'd suggested it would be better to do it at her house; although I pointed out it would be more convenient to just talk in her office, I felt obliged to travel there once she emailed me saying she would love to lure me out to the lakeside with sweet lemonade and a garden about to bloom.

When I arrived that Thursday afternoon she looked as effortlessly put together as usual, even in jeans and a bell-sleeved angora jumper, the kind that hadn't pilled or grown fuzzy from wear. She flung open the doors that led from her kitchen to the garden and swimming lake.

'Everything is about to burst because of all the rain,' she said, fingering a pot of mint by the deck's edge. She brought it up to my face and I took a good sniff. 'It's godly. Look at the pink rosebuds, all tight and puckered now – soon they will open, like willing mouths. Those vines round the front of the patio simply explode in summer, a verdant symphony of leaves and swollen grapes. In the winter, I neglect the whole thing, leave all my feelings about nature to rot. Then, as spring approaches, it takes over my life like a newborn. I'm on my knees trying to coax everything to its full potential,' she enthused. 'We're all existing in cycles we have very little control over. It's worth remembering that everything has its season and every phase is only that – a phase.'

I felt that she was trying to ignite my interest, but I attempted to ignore the romantic way she spoke about nature. I focused instead on the hard, oiled wood of her garden chairs and smelt the sweet waft of the natural water of her lake, just starting to wake up for spring.

Everything was just beginning, I decided, seeing the pages of my work spread out in front of her, the physical manifestation that I was writing something that was coming together, a small part of a larger whole that had a momentum both beyond me and inside of me. Hearing Sofie talk about my writing with gravity was both overwhelming and intoxicating.

She shifted the paper around in front of her while we looked over the swimming lake.

'It's actually much harder to take care of than a chlorine-filled swimming pool, because of the complex filtration system that stops the water from going green,' she told me. 'Even the slightest change or flaw in the system,' she tapped the side of her lemonade glass with a polished fingernail, 'and the whole thing could turn putrid.'

To me, the water appeared so clear you could drink from it. The lake was always talked about by her students, who said that if you were lucky you might be invited round for a summer swim.

'It's beautiful,' I said. 'Did you do it all yourself?'

She looked pleased to have been asked.

'I did! Back when I bought the house, the lake was a green swamp. It cost a lot of money to make it what it is now. But sometimes,' she said, brushing an invisible hair from her forehead, a self-conscious gesture that made me think she was being sincere, 'I think it was the best thing I've ever done.'

I looked back at my pages, wanting to move the conversation on. She seemed to clock my distraction and picked up my work, shuffling it in front of her. I worried I hadn't been effusive enough about our surroundings. She took a cap off a pen and started working her way through the pages, telling me where I'd droned on too long and where I could've been clearer.

'Sometimes your sentences are too long,' she told me, 'and the reader will lose the thread of what you're saying. When there's tension, when something bad is happening, a shorter sentence works a lot better.' Her lips pulled together. She frowned, striking something out on the page. 'You don't need this bit, isn't it obvious now it's been cut?'

I readily agreed without bothering to reread the sentence. The right answer was obvious when it was presented to you. But the trick was in getting there.

'Apart from these points,' she said, 'you're onto something really special. I like where it's going, and the choices your character has made. It's clever what you did, having her decide to stay with her husband only to end up being hounded by her obsessive boyfriend. Like a kind of gender-flipped *Fatal Attraction*.' She smiled at me. 'It's starting to feel real, isn't it?'

I didn't know whether she meant the story or the idea of it becoming a book, but either way her confidence in me was infectious.

'I want to make it good,' I said. I don't know why I said such a banal thing.

She put her pen down.

'For your first novel, everything is up for grabs. Everything you've ever experienced. You can put anything you want in here.' She gestured at the page. 'You only get that feeling once.' She smiled at me and complimented the cut of my top. I told her it was one that she'd given me.

'I know. There's plenty more where that came from.' She put the stack of pages to one side and a breeze licked at the edges. Before I could reach a hand out, the wind picked a couple of pages up and towards the lake. I exclaimed and slammed a hand down on the rest of the pile, watching as the pages floated down towards the water, ready to be subsumed.

'Never mind,' Sofie said. 'I assume you have copies?'

I nodded, looking around for something to weight the paper down with.

'Do you want to have a look at some more things I'm getting rid of?'

'Oh no, I couldn't,' I mumbled.

She reached across the table and put her hand over mine, which I left flat on the manuscript like it was playing dead. It's happening, I thought, and I don't know how to stop it. My skin prickled with electric dread. She patted it a couple of times and then told me to follow her.

In her dressing room, she told me she was just so pleased that her old clothes would be going to a good home. It made her feel better about all the money she wasted on things she hardly wore. She went out to the bedroom and came back in with an armful of clothes.

'You should try these,' she said, 'while you're here.' I envied the way her thin, gold bracelet fell down her slender wrist. She put the pile down on her velvet chair and glanced in one of the mirrors to readjust her hair, then saw me watching her. She smiled sweetly. 'You have to get rid of your money somehow,' she said.

'I wanted to ask you,' I started, then stopped. I was aware of my own stupidity even as I held her attention. 'Did you really find a hair in one of your juices?' She was peering down at a loose thread on the neckline of a slip dress, making a face as she tried to pluck it between her thumb and forefinger.

'I did,' she said, 'and it felt better to bring it to the kitchen's attention rather than pretend it had never happened. Imagine if it had been a less understanding customer.'

'I just wish you had come to me,' I said. 'I would've sorted you out with replacement drinks. One of the girls there was upset.'

She gave a half-nod as I spoke, then gestured for me to try on the dress. I looked around for somewhere to get changed.

'It's okay,' she said, 'you can try it on here.' She perched herself next to the clothes she'd put on the chair, making a show of sorting through them rather than looking at me. 'I'm sorry your colleagues were upset, anyway. I only told the truth. Really, I've done them a favour, because if that kind of thing happened a lot, with other people's juices, the whole operation could be shut down. Then you might not have a job.'

'I don't want it to be my job forever.' I was pulling off my jeans as I spoke, still holding the dress in one hand, embarrassed by the cheap cotton underwear that left red indentations on my skin.

'Exactly,' she said. 'I was just trying to help.'

'What did you do with it? The juice?' I hopped on one foot as I tried to put my leg through the neck of the dress.

She looked up and told me I'd have to put it over my head.

'Here,' she said, coming towards me and lifting the fabric over my head with my arms outstretched to the ceiling. As the material passed over my face, I had the uncomfortable sensation that she was studying my body, that my breasts were pressed out towards her, and

I wanted to readjust my underwear. But in a moment, the dress had covered me as though nothing had happened.

'I poured the juice down the sink,' she said.

'You took a photo of it first.'

I took a step towards the mirror away from her. It clung to me in all the wrong places and reminded me that although in theory our bodies were a similar size, in reality the difference was enormous. I was sure Sofie thought the same, as she didn't immediately comment on the dress, saying instead:

'I took a photo of the juice first, yes.'

'Don't you think it could have been your hair?'

She barked a laugh.

'How could my hair have found its way into a sealed bottle? Unless I'd been stalking you at your workplace? This has really bothered you, hasn't it?' she said. Then, softening, she went on, 'Look, I'm sorry you're so upset. It's one of those unpleasant things that have to happen sometimes, to make things better in the long run. Like paying your taxes or getting a cervical smear.'

I wasn't sure why it mattered so much, when the job was so stupid. But it bothered me, stepping into the world of someone who had no concept of what I actually did all day and how hard the women in the juice kitchen worked. It bothered me how little she understood it, and how desperate I was to not care about what happened there, and to be accepted into this kind of life.

I opened my mouth to say this, to tell her that even though my job was small, it was only people like her who made it feel like that. The rest of the time, when we were in there working, it felt like we were making something of value. It was only when we saw who bought what we made that it felt stupid, because they were the kind of people who'd buy anything if the label on the bottle had the right words on it.

Instead, I said nothing, and shrugged at my own reflection.

'Do you like it?' she asked me, finally turning her attention to the dress.

I wanted to keep it just to marvel at it, but I said, 'No, I don't think it looks quite right.'

'No, maybe not. Things just aren't made with the same quality any more.' The loose thread was now sitting on the curve of my chest, and she reached out and pinched it between her fingers again. I drew in a shocked breath as her hand grazed my skin, as though I could pull my body further away from her. Her fingers still holding the thread, she turned her wrist so that her hand moved slowly down the fabric that covered my breast. Gently, she smoothed the satin, her fingers tracing the outline of my bra.

She said, 'It's a wonder the whole dress didn't unravel with this kind of craftmanship.' Then she looked up at me and pressed her thumb against my nipple. Through the lace of my bra, it stood up to attention. I watched her hand as though it was on someone else's body.

By the time I raised my head, she had released me and turned away to pick through the rest of the clothes. My body stood in numb shock, my stomach sick and heavy. I tried to think of a way to leave immediately, without undressing and without goodbyes.

'I'm sorry about the whole situation,' she said. 'You know how much I love the juices. Now, what might you like to try on next?'

Eight

Jo

It went like this: the first time Jo met Sofie Muller was when she came in for her interview for her undergraduate degree. She took the train from King's Cross with a sandwich her mother had wrapped up in paper for her. She ate it as soon as she boarded, sick to her stomach, but enjoying the mulch of white bread in her mouth. Her shoes were too tight but highly polished and on the table in front of her was a novel she'd read several times. It was one of Sofie's, and because she'd mentioned it in her personal essay on her application, she was worried she'd be asked about it. She'd written notes in the margins and circled important words and phrases. On a page near the back, she had a list of words she had to look up in the dictionary.

When she arrived, she walked from the train station to the campus. She had a letter with her, inviting her to the interview with her time slot. She was going to get a tour and speak with two members of the faculty. This was because she had applied for a joint honours degree, the only way her mother would let her do a course that included Creative Writing. The other half would be English Literature, a small concession.

Jo had never met an author before, but she imagined that they wore tweed jackets and permanent frowns, buried beneath piles of books and facial hair. She was therefore surprised when she was sitting outside the Creative Writing office, her satchel balanced carefully on her lap, and a woman opened the door wearing a black polo neck and leather boots underneath a mid-length skirt, the kind of outfit Jo had seen in magazines. Her hair was pulled back, smoothed away from her temples to emphasise her strikingly beautiful face. Sofie introduced herself, pointing to the novel that Jo was still holding in her hand, and Jo realised she'd been staring.

'Oh!' she said, before moving to get up from her chair.

Sofie laughed.

She could tell Sofie was used to this kind of reaction, sitting down behind her desk with an amused expression on her face.

'Tell me about the last five books you read,' Sofie said.

Jo looked down at Sofie's novel and swallowed. It was the only one she could think of, so she said, 'I loved the story so much, I've read it three times.'

While she said this, Sofie picked up her admissions essay; Jo recognised her own handwriting. Sofie nodded without looking up.

'But what else have you read recently?'

Jo could feel the dampness underneath her shirt and she wracked her brains for something intelligent to say. She listed a few Victorian novels.

'And do you only read writers that are either sitting in front of you or dead?'

Jo tripped over the words, 'No, no, of course not,' but couldn't think of anything else to say.

Sofie put the essay down. Her self-satisfied smile was long gone now, and she looked dreadfully bored.

'Was Tess seduced, or was she raped?'

Jo gazed at her mutely.

'Tess of the d'Urbervilles. Was she a victim or a slut?'

Jo recoiled at the word, recovered herself and started talking about the different versions that Hardy had written, the passages he'd added in or left out, what he might have thought about a fallen woman.

'I don't give a shit what Hardy thought,' said Sofie. 'What do *you* think?'

'I . . . it's hard to decide what I think until I know what Hardy intended. But if I had to say, then Tess was obviously a victim of circumstance. Of society and nature.'

Sofie nodded thoughtfully. 'You don't think she had any agency at all?'

While Jo considered this, she glanced out of the window behind Sofie Muller. There was a tree that would blossom in the spring. Right now it was bare, its branches looming towards the window like sinister fingers.

'Even if she was seduced, she was still very much a victim. And no, I don't think she had much agency at all.'

Sofie leaned forward, crossing her arms.

'And what about the ending? Was it the ultimate feminist act?' Sofie mimicked cutting her own throat, and Jo realised she was testing her to see if she'd finished the book.

Jo shook her head, wondering if Sofie would call herself a feminist. 'No, because she murdered her perpetrator for another man, not for herself.'

Sofie seemed satisfied with this.

'You might consider reading some more contemporary writers, especially women. The Victorians won't show you what you're up against.'

'Up against?' Jo repeated.

Sofie picked up a pile of papers and pulled out a few pages that had been stapled together.

'Your writing sample was exceptional and I will be offering you a place. As long as you promise to worry less about what male writers think. Especially those that have been dead for almost a century.'

* * *

It was hard to remember how it all started after that. Jo attended the lectures she was meant to and, as if a door in her mind had been opened, she wrote constantly. She read everything Sofie gave her and spent time in her office talking about each book. In her second year Sofie became her personal tutor, and while she struggled to make many close friends in her halls of residence, she found it easy to talk to Sofie. She wasn't intimidated any more.

One day, without thinking, Jo had complimented Sofie on her cashmere scarf, and Sofie had unwound it from her neck while they were talking and given it to her. Jo tried to refuse it, but Sofie pretended she hadn't heard. Later, Jo went home and laid the scarf out on her bed like a throw. She saw a couple of hairs that belonged to Sofie and pulled them from the fabric. She put her face down into the scarf to smell Sofie's perfume, and that's when she realised she was desperately in love.

It had been Jo, hadn't it? The first one to admit that something else was going on. She was at Sofie's house for one of her tutorials and started to probe into Sofie's personal life.

'Do you have a boyfriend?' she'd said.

Sofie had cackled, throwing her head back; and then, in a gesture that felt somehow pitying, had tucked a strand of hair behind Jo's ear. After a couple of years of knowing each other, Jo was used to the overfamiliarity, but this time she took Sofie's hand and held it against her cheek.

From that moment, she was lost forever.

Yes, even now it went like this: Sofie answered her door without surprise. Jo had rehearsed it all in her head on the way over. She would tell Sofie she was going to reply to the email from the journalist. She had to. She couldn't think about anything else: all those young students, afraid. She was the only person in the world who could really verify what was being said. But when she saw Sofie's face, it felt easier to smile and follow her through to the immaculate kitchen, look out at the pond and surrender to that feeling of comfortable familiarity. She took the gin and tonic with perfectly curled cucumber that was handed to her. She laughed at Sofie's jokes about spending all day on her knees in the garden.

Sofie crunched on her own cucumber garnish and said, 'Days like this remind me why I work in front of a computer. I wasn't built for hard work, not really.' She grinned, waiting for Jo to rebuke her.

Jo just smiled.

'I'd rather spend a day in a garden like this than those days at the office where you feel self-conscious even going to get a glass of water.'

'You do?'

Jo knew she would never understand, because she'd always worked where she'd been in charge, one way or another.

'It takes a special kind of energy to be surrounded by people who want things from you,' she said. 'Not necessarily your work, your output, you could do that anywhere. More like, your compliance. Your smile and acquiescence to the stupid things people say, how you have to go along with conversations with your colleagues when really you'd rather just do your work or anything else.'

'Your male colleagues, you mean? Who knew writing little tweets would be that bad?'

They were standing by the pond. Jo had been at her desk all day, she'd pointed out, so she didn't want to sit down just yet.

'I never told you this,' she said, 'but in my last job, I sat next to one of the managing partners.' She looked at Sofie, watching the lines on her face settle into the story. 'And there was something I couldn't quite put my finger on about him, but I always found him slightly unsettling. The way he'd look at you as he talked for hours about the various projects he'd been working on, and where he lived and what his wife thought of the new bathroom. He had this air about him, like he was so eager to capture your attention and keep it. It never went any further than that, but I found it uncomfortable, having to manage this expectation that every day we'd have these meaningless conversations and I would have to smile and nod and pretend to find him terribly interesting.'

Sofie sighed. 'That sounds onerous.'

'God, it was. It's hard to explain because it sounds like nothing. But it took so much energy to have to pretend all the time. It was only later that I found out he'd harassed two of my female colleagues at the Christmas party. And his wife was someone he'd met at work, twenty years younger.' Sofie pulled a face as Jo continued: 'I just couldn't stop imagining that she'd been in a similar position to me. That after a while, she just sort of gave in to the attention. Or maybe she did genuinely fall in love with him, which now I think about it is even worse.'

'People fall in love with the most odious people. It's worth remembering that,' said Sofie, her eyes twinkling.

Jo laughed and drained her drink. She held up the glass to an imaginary waiter and Sofie swatted her hand.

'All right, another.'

Sometimes Jo worried that she spent so much time alone that she'd forget how to be interesting to other people, especially someone like Sofie who prized good conversation and vibrant energy. But it was easy when Sofie poured generous drinks and they stood in the cool spring air talking about people they hated.

It was only when Sofie grabbed Jo's arm with a hand that was cold and wet from the gin glass that Jo realised she'd failed. She had only ever been interesting in one way.

'I can't,' Jo said, as Sofie leaned in and brushed her lips against the shoulder of her T-shirt. 'That's why I came.'

Sofie released her grasp from Jo's arm and looked at her with a grim satisfaction.

'You came to tell me you can't?'

The ice in Sofie's glass rattled like applause.

'I just don't think that kind of thing can happen between us any more. Not now. We stopped doing all that.'

'Is this about that journalist?' asked Sofie. 'Because you seemed pretty okay about it last time you were here.'

Jo shifted her weight from one foot to another.

'You know I'm the only one who can tell the truth,' she said. 'I'm the only one, really, who can add anything of import to this conversation.'

Sofie snorted.

'And what exactly would you add? That we helped each other with our work while we were married?'

'Not just that.' Jo could hear that her voice had risen an octave, in her determination to be heard. 'What about the students? What about their work?'

Sofie took a controlled sip from her drink.

'You can't really believe we did anything wrong? We only used small kernels, little nothings from stories that weren't going to make it. Where does any idea come from? Don't all writers steal?'

'Yes,' Jo said, 'I suppose so.'

'You pull at that thread, that way of working, and there's a lot that starts to unravel.' Sofie was satisfied with her own argument, and the way she slapped a hand against her arm in self-congratulation was all too familiar.

'But it was never just a kernel, was it?' said Jo. 'It was more than that.'

She couldn't always tell if Sofie deliberately mis-remembered, or whether so much time had passed that she really did believe what she told herself. Because it was whole drafts of work from writing classes, pages and pages of plot, too, that eventually became Sofie's prize-winning novels. The two of them did the legwork, sure, but did that make it okay?

'We always had a good partnership, you know that,' Sofie said. 'But you also know that I wrote those bloody books. And if you want to say any different, then you're going to have to face up to your own role in all of this.'

Jo had been banking on some kind of threat. It was almost a relief to finally hear one. And so what? After all these years, what did Jo care if it was finally all said out loud? Sofie thought Jo had somewhere to fall from, but she had nothing left wrapped up in fiction. It was Sofie's throne to lose. It was all Sofie. She said nothing.

'Do you really think without me, you'd ever have had a book published?' continued Sofie.

'No, probably not.'

Sofie made a sweeping gesture with her free hand as if to say: There it is, those are the facts.

'But that's not the whole story, is it?' said Jo. 'It's only part of it.'

Sofie looked back out at the garden.

'The whole story is overrated,' she said wearily. 'Whenever you read a book, or someone tells you something that happened to them, do you think you ever get the whole story? Never. It's always a little piece of it. And humans are wired that way, we're better like that. Sometimes life is easier when you just have your part of the story, the part that makes sense.'

'Sofie, sometimes you do talk an awful lot of shit.'

Sofie smiled without turning to face her.

'I do! I do it every day, you know, in front of the students. I just say the first thing that comes into my head and most of the time they genuinely seem to think it's sound advice. All writing advice is like that, in a sense. Anything can be true if you say it in the right way, with enough conviction.' Sofie crooked her fingers into air quotes. 'You just say "Write every day, write when you can, write before work, before dawn, after work, until dawn." When the truth is, there are as many types of writing and writers as there are different people, so why does anyone need advice on the mechanics of doing it, other than to just sit down and get it done?'

That's the kind of secret that could take down a whole writing programme, thought Jo. The best piece of advice and biggest truism

Sofie ever offered was the way she signed off every email to students with the words: keep writing.

Sofie made it all seem so effortless and easy, like they could just forget the whole thing if they wanted. 'What are we going to do then?' she asked her.

Sofie said, 'I'm not going to beg you to love me again. I can accept that that ship has sailed, even if I'm still stuck at the harbour. But you have to let this go. Can't you see? You're in a unique position. You can forgive yourself for your part in this, by forgiving me. Oh, I want to take your hair in my hands, but I won't.'

'To drag me round the garden?'

'To soothe you like a child. To tell you how much I care. And to plead with you. To ask you to please take pity on an old woman with only a few good years left of her career.' Sofie blinked at her, her eyes wide and glassy.

Jo shook her head, but Sofie was undeterred.

'You know I'm old. I've got twenty years on you. Soon, I'll retire and no one will give a shit about Sofie bloody Muller. And maybe there'll be plenty of people who'll be happy about that, but all I want is my last few years. Please don't take them away.'

'I can't remember the last time you ever asked me for anything,' said Jo.

'I gave you a gift once. People read your writing and loved it. And I did that, it was *me*.' Sofie's voice grew louder. 'If that mattered to you at all, if *I* matter to you at all, you'll know this thing needs to just be left alone.'

Jo realised her legs were shaking, but she didn't want Sofie to notice.

'I might have to go soon. The gin has got to me.'

'You do get it though, don't you? What's happening here?' Sofie took her arm again. 'Someone's spotted a few similarities, and that's enough to take away the fact that I've helped countless people get published. I've spent years of my life, dedicated most of my career, to reading other people's work and helping them create true works of art. I could easily have just sat in this house and written ten more novels than I did. But I wanted to help others.'

It was true, in a sense. And this kind of truth made Jo feel special because she was the only one who could tell it. The way Sofie spoke to her, so desperately, reminded her of the simple fact that Jo was the only one who had the power to save her. And even though love sometimes felt like rage, it was a powerful thing to save other people, instead of just saving yourself.

As though sensing her wavering, Sofie pulled Jo towards her, drawing a soft hand across her hair. 'I helped you, too, didn't I? I know you felt like we were doing something wrong, but it was really nothing. We took some terrible ideas and saved them from a graveyard.' She leaned in and kissed her forehead. 'We wrote the most beautiful books.'

Jo didn't know how beautiful they ever were. To her they felt contrived, mechanical; but sometimes, when Sofie let Jo get carried away and write the things she wanted, there were elements of beauty. She had the sense, although she'd never vocalised it, that Sofie had been searching for almost ten years for a replacement, someone who could do the butchering and the beauty the way Jo had. But stealing and spinning was an art.

Yes, the money was good, the warm glow of satisfaction, the way Sofie strutted about the house, elated, when they'd finished something successful, the way they both vibrated with excitement – it was heady. But it had all become too much. After a while, Sofie seemed to resent the instrumental part Jo played, convinced herself she could do it all on her own. After Jo left and then returned, she had told her as much: she was furious. It was over, they couldn't do this together any more. And Jo had been so relieved.

But now time had passed and Sofie had nothing to show for it. She needed her again. She was vulnerable, desperate, a little girl who'd awoken in the night to damp sheets and called for her mother. And Jo's money had run out, after all.

Into Jo's silence Sofie said, 'I'll do anything you want, JoJo. You should have anything you want.' She took Jo's face in her hands, kissed her nose and the tips of her ears. 'I could help you with another book of your own, is that what you'd like? About anything you want, I can help you. I can make it big. You could have a break from office life, you could make the world beautiful with your writing.'

That was when Sofie nestled against her and said what Jo had heard many times before, making it feel as though outside of Sofie's orbit she had no value, no creative worth, no love or affection or care to offer anyone else at all.

'I'd be nothing without you,' Sofie said. 'I'd be nothing.'

A statement from Jocasta Franklin:

I have been shocked and appalled at the recent claims made against my ex-wife, Sofie Muller, in relation to allegations of plagiarism from former students in her works of fiction.

Sofie has dedicated her career to helping others create unique and meaningful work that fulfils the potential of each individual student. During my own time as her student, she helped to shape and realise the novel I would go on to publish. I owe my career to her guidance, tuition, and relentless dedication to the craft of my writing.

While other students may feel differently, any similarities between early pieces I wrote and Sofie's published work are purely coincidental, and the lack of concrete evidence across all allegations is testament to this.

Fiction is purely that – a fiction. Anyone looking hard enough will find plot points, words and ideas that bear an anecdotal similarity to another writer's work. This is part of a long history of humans telling stories that are unique but universal. It is nothing more sinister than that.

If these allegations gain credibility from an online jury, we set a dangerous precedent for art and inspiration all over the country. What is at stake is not just the fate of creative freedom in fiction, but of, in particular, women who dare to stand up and tell their stories in print – and help others to do so.

I urge everyone to dismiss a carefully crafted conspiracy aimed at tearing down a woman in power and instead consider a person who has dedicated her life to creating and guiding others to create true works of art.

Nine

Alice

The day after I tried on Sofie's clothes, I was back at the juice kitchen. The longer I worked there, the harder the work became. The demands on my time grew: it was expected that I would work long hours, that even when I was away from the kitchen I would answer emails and take calls from the delivery company. Despite Molly's absenteeism, her business seemed to be growing in momentum, gathering the kind of success that even she struggled to take credit for. Those of us who were on-site throughout the week marvelled at the demand, the growing need for self-improvement that fuelled cleanse after cleanse.

But the more frantic the work became, the less I felt able to muster up the energy to do it.

I found myself going to bed and telling myself that in those little seven or eight hours, Molly couldn't possibly expect a reply. But then at seven thirty in the morning I'd be on the phone again, negotiating with a courier about a pack of juices that hadn't arrived in Knightsbridge on time. The three-day shelf life gave everything a sense of urgency that was both real and overblown, and Olena and I would often just top up bottles from out-of-date produce to save on time.

Sometimes I would sit in the back office of the kitchen and feel amazed that so much of my brain space could be taken up by something as stupid as fruit and water. As my writing deadlines became more urgent, the hours I worked there increased, and I felt one bleed into the other. I wrote on my lunchbreak while I watched Olena fill bottles. I spoke to Molly on the phone while she went from workout class to party to hotel. I constantly left things to the last minute, running out of packing tape for delivery boxes, stickers for the expiry dates and produce for the juices. I ran on a strange kind of energy, safe in the knowledge that the world wouldn't implode if rich people didn't drink their spinach and kale drink that tasted like pond water, while trying to stay high on the idea that what I did was very important because people told me so.

Olena still stayed late every evening to sit and look at her secret phone, but I would leave as soon as possible to try and get back to my work in progress. I knew it was always there, waiting for me, and every hour I spent working on something else cost me dearly in terms of word count.

That day, I saw Sofie had placed another order. I felt anxious when I saw it on the spreadsheet, but decided not to tell Olena who the juice pack was for. Instead, I labelled and ordered the bottles precisely, careful to avoid my fingerprints messing up the neat, glossy appearance. I gently lined up the rectangular plastic bottles, waiting for the juice to be ready to fill them. There had been a shortage of spinach earlier in the day, so everyone was staying late to catch up on the orders.

I was anxious to leave on time, but when I saw the juicers groaning under the weight of produce at gone seven o'clock, and the fibrous patties of vegetable remnants discarded in the bins, only half full, I realised it was going to take a while.

I was sitting in the office opening and closing the spreadsheet, trying to work out how long it would take me to pack all the bottles in the right order to the right people. One customer lived in a famous block of flats in London that had a glass pool suspended in the sky, an aquatic bridge that represented new extremes of excess.

What did those people need juice for anyway? Wasn't it enough that they lived in one of the most sought-after locations in the country? How much did they buy on a whim and leave to slowly curdle?

'It's okay, Alice, I can do it for you,' Olena said, standing in the doorway to the office and snapping on her plastic gloves. 'If you want to go home. Half of the bottles are ready, and the other half I can do, if you lay it out for me.'

I didn't doubt it, but I'd been explicitly told never to let Olena do this. Just in case something didn't quite translate, just in case the orders got missed or switched and it was put on the women who weren't native English speakers. But I had someone I wanted to see before the day was over, and Olena's English was excellent, I told myself.

I printed out the spreadsheet and packed the juices that were ready into the correct cool bags. Then I laid out the empty bottles in the right order for each address with the right bag and label, making it clear what needed to be filled and packed. I booked the courier for later that night and instructed Olena what should go where. I looked at her, worried.

'It's straightforward, right? It should be fine?'

She nodded.

'It makes no difference to me. I'll be staying late anyway, to wait for the spinach.'

I thanked her.

'You promise to go home and use the time to write something that matters?' she said.

I laid out the label for the last delivery: Sofie Muller. Later that night, she would have an abundance of almond milk and beetroot and carrot juice. Maybe her urine would turn pink and she would worry that she'd got her period unexpectedly. Without wanting to, I imagined her inserting her fingers into her vagina only for them to come out clean. It was strange that as I left and waved goodbye to Olena I thought of that. Now I couldn't stop imagining Sofie in these kinds of situations, and wondering what she had done with other students, like shameful intrusive thoughts. They both intrigued and disgusted me. And of course, the first thing I thought of when I left Sofie's house was Walt. I felt a lump rising in my throat every time I thought of him and how I had been so coldly dismissive.

Yes, I was meant to leave now and write. But how could I think of anything else? Leaving the juice kitchen early that day seemed as inconsequential a decision as what to have for dinner. I didn't pay much mind to Olena, or what she was doing for me. It only meant something later: when the juices never turned up to Sofie's door, when she called Molly to tell her that her order was missing, when it became clear I hadn't been there.

I knocked on Walt's door. On the way to his halls, I had rehearsed all the things I wanted to say in my head. At the very least I could just say sorry.

No answer came, so I walked out of the building and headed for the green space where we'd walked so many times. The spring air was warm, tickling the fabric of my dress. It was one of Sofie's, but now I felt there was nothing so glamorous about it after all. I looked down at the colourful print and felt embarrassed. It was sickening to imagine her body inside the clothes I wore, and I suddenly wanted to be rid of them all. I couldn't stop thinking about her hand on me, how many hands she'd laid on others.

Then I saw him. A lone figure in a wool duffel coat, smoking a cigarette behind the building. I knew it was Walt from the way he flicked his wrist and tilted his head when he saw me.

'You don't smoke,' I said, leaning my back against the wall beside him.

'You don't talk to me.' He took a drag like he'd found a long-lost love. He held the cigarette out to me but I shook my head.

'They just make me cough.'

'God, Alice, you can be so posh sometimes.'

I bridled.

He looked out to the trees that converged around the lake.

'So, what do you want? I'm not going for another swim if that's what you're thinking about.'

'How are you? Really?' I said.

'Never better. In fact, all I need is a phone call from my mother and the day really will be complete.'

I started to nibble at a hangnail.

'Why does she call you so much? Is she worried about you?'

He flicked the ash from the end of his cigarette with his thumb, thought about it, and took another drag.

'She's lonely. She wants me to come home.'

'What are you going to do?'

He scowled at me. 'Not that.'

'Would it really be so bad?'

He dropped his cigarette butt and ground it out under his shoe, then picked it back up again and held it in his hand.

'It's not good to litter, Alice.' He looked at it in his palm. 'My childhood was so mundane and awful in so many ways, I had to dedicate time to learning how to appreciate very little. It's pretty easy, once you learn to treasure the stupidest things. Now, there's nothing in the world that's so enticing that it can tempt me away from small joys. Twice a year I have a cigarette. Once on my birthday and once on the anniversary of my dad's death.'

He had written several pieces about the loss of his father, and they were always difficult to read. I wanted to say something, to express sympathy, but stopped myself as I knew he hated platitudes.

'People think the cigarette thing is stupid,' he continued. 'But I think it's very sophisticated of me to be so abstemious.' He balled up his fist and put the cigarette end in his coat pocket. 'This last year has been pretty shit. But I can still have my little smoke.'

'Walt.'

I touched his shoulder. The wool of his coat was soft and threadbare, and I thought it was the kind of coat that was brought out year after year for comfort rather than warmth. I wondered if it had been his father's.

He didn't look at me.

'What do you want, Alice?'

'I'm sorry,' I said. 'That's the least of it. I should've listened to you. I made a horrible mistake.'

He looked shocked.

'I've waited so long to hear you say that.'

'I did all the wrong things,' I whispered.

He searched my face.

'What did she do to you?' he said suddenly.

I rubbed the goosebumps on my arms.

'Oh, no, nothing. Nothing like that.'

'What is it then?'

'It's just, I believe you now.'

He slipped his coat off without saying anything and put it over my shoulders.

'Tell me why,' he said.

But I couldn't.

I held the coat over my shoulders and squeezed the soft wool in my hands. I breathed in the smell of him: sweet and earthy.

'I wish things were different,' I said. 'I don't know what to do now.' I looked up at his sweet face, the curl of hair over his forehead. 'I just, I wanted to know. Why didn't you tell someone what was going on sooner?'

He let out a cold laugh.

I let myself reach out a hand and touch his hair. I had tried so hard to get away from him, but something always pulled me back. It would be clichéd to say he felt like home, especially when we'd both come here to escape ours. But it felt something like that: familiar, easy.

'I thought at the end of this course I'd have a book deal,' he said. 'That's the kind of thing she promised. I thought I'd be on my way. I thought I'd found something, even, with you. But it turns out it was just another year of my life – wasted.'

'No, no, it's not a waste, it hasn't been a waste.' My heart lifted when he mentioned our relationship.

'Maybe not. I've been writing a little bit. I don't want to fail the entire year.'

'What have you been writing about?' I asked.

'Nothing much.'

I thought about his story of the woman murdered in the woods and tried to imagine what new levels of bloodied violence his disquieted mind had conjured up now. But for once, I didn't want to talk about writing. I took a deep breath.

'I found something with you, too,' I said. 'I know it's been a bad year, but I'm so happy I met you.'

He flinched like he'd been hit. I took a step back from him.

'It's just, Walt, I think you've been so brave.'

He smiled stiffly and asked for his coat back. He was standing up straight now, like a wild animal, alert, about to flee. I handed back the coat and he turned to walk away, but then swung back and came up close to me.

'I told you this would happen, that you'd believe me eventually, too late. But you didn't give a shit about me then, did you?' His voice became louder. 'I needed you, and you weren't there.'

'I know that,' I told him. 'You should get mad at me, hit me, if that helps.'

'Are you *high*, Alice? I'm not going to hit you.' He was shouting now, waving the coat like a flag. 'After months, you think I'm "brave"?'

He looked at me, waiting for an answer, but I didn't say anything. It was true. I had been weak, and now I only wanted him to care about me again. I reached my hands out to quieten him and he tried to pull away. I stroked his neck and cheek and then leant forward to kiss him. He reached a hand up to meet mine and breathed out, letting me pull him into me. Then just as suddenly, he stepped back.

'No,' he said quietly. 'You've done enough. I might be brave, but I think you're a fucking coward.' I could tell by his face that he meant it. He turned and walked away.

The third phase

One

Jo

It happened just like that. The article was published at the end of the Easter holidays, just ahead of a new term, which must have been deliberate. It would be less crushing to have the fallout happen when the university was deserted and Sofie wasn't expected to attend any classes.

Then, one thing followed another. Anonymous Reddit posts about Sofie, written by several different users, were unearthed. *Can anyone give me advice about my writing tutor? Has anyone else ever been harassed by Sofie Muller?* they asked, over and over again, crowdsourcing complaints as though they'd found a bit of glass in their breakfast cereal. They'd been appearing solidly for months, but no one had noticed them until now.

It was during this time Jo realised that Sofie might have been right: it was easier and better when things were left alone.

Sofie was manic, calling her at all times of the day and night, asking her over and over to help her. Jo felt protective and wanted to shield her from what was unfolding, but at the same time she thought often of how quickly things had changed. Only a few weeks before, her whole life was entirely separate from the drama that surrounded Sofie. Somehow, she'd been pulled back in and had become the leader of Sofie's defence. She'd thought that one letter that she published online would be her first and last statement on the matter, but it was just the beginning. Now, she was spending time rallying other academics, writers and publishers to defend not only Sofie's reputation but the freedom of creativity. She wrote emails, made phone calls, implored every last powerful friend of Sofie's she could remember to help.

She went to work as though none of this was happening. She didn't explain to her colleagues that she'd suddenly found herself at the centre of an online publishing shitstorm, and it amazed her every day that it never touched them. What felt so central to the whole world only affected a tiny corner of the book world. She typed out her marketing social media posts and told herself it didn't matter, but every tweet and blog and Reddit thread enraged her. They appeared too quickly for her to lobby for them all to be taken down.

She felt sorry for Sofie in a way she'd never imagined she could, even though she suspected the whole thing would soon blow over. It was in her power to stay calm and act properly where Sofie couldn't, so she told her what to do and what to say, and advised her to stay off social media. Jo would sort it out.

The day a group of feminist writers and academics posted a public letter of defence signed by 125 prominent people, led by Booker-nominated author and friend Eleanor Crippon, Jo told Sofie it would all be over soon. But it also happened to be the same day Sofie was temporarily suspended from the university. The timing was impeccable.

Jo, of course, thought about the girl, Alice, the one who'd appeared that night at Sofie's house. It was Alice she thought of first when she read the posts about harassment online. How could it not be? Her hot little face, her cheeks like bruised plums. All the bloom of youth in Sofie's hands. It was hard not to think of, and she reasoned this was why she read and re-read those threads over and over again. Most of the replies to these posts were from students who were laughing at Sofie, taking none of it very seriously. *She's old as fuck,* they wrote, *but good for her. She gave a good go of it and the students only had to say no thank you ma'am.*

Others were less flippant. *It hardly surprises me,* they wrote. *She never touched me, but it makes sense because she never made any secret of having favourites and inviting them over to her house to get drunk. I had no idea that favourites meant touching people up, but could I honestly say it surprised me? About as much as those police dogs who mauled their neighbour's cats to death. It's just in their nature.*

I put in a complaint about her years ago, another wrote. *But I guess they didn't want to aggravate her, because allegedly she had a couple of very tempting offers from other universities. The way they acted was as though in exchange for her loyalty to them, they'd given her immunity. I thought it was messed up, but I felt totally powerless. It felt like there was no point saying anything at all.*

From each post came a new allegation, anonymous but compellingly written, given that the posters were mostly writers who had excelled under Sofie's tutelage.

I went to her house and went swimming in her pool. I hadn't brought a costume to wear, and she told me I could just go in my underwear. It didn't feel weird until later when she plied me with red wine and said we should go upstairs. I followed, without really thinking anything of it, and after coming back from the toilet found her naked on the bed. She asked me to join her. When I tell you I ran out of that house faster than a deer on speed . . . well, forget the analogy. I fucking ran.

This one gave Jo a jolt. She couldn't imagine Sofie doing something so brazen. Jo always made sure to go out on the evenings when students were around, because it made her so uncomfortable – their optimism, their love for writing, the way they flattered Sofie. She couldn't imagine any of the interactions these people described, but that only made them more disturbing.

But she baulked at the mention of 'favourites'. She thought about them over and over, in the shower and on walks by the river. They'd signed up for one of the most prestigious courses in the country and then had their feelings hurt. But Sofie helped countless students get published. And her style of pedagogy was no secret! Jo wanted to shout, with righteous anger. It had never been a secret.

Then, an email landed directly in her inbox, a week into the new term and five days into Sofie's suspension. It was from a boy. It surprised her, but not as much as she might have thought. She wondered if it was the one that Sofie had mentioned last year, who she'd been enamoured with and then decided against. Jo read and re-read his name, trying to imagine he was a real person. She opened the email at work, the smell of forlorn coffee and printer cartridges filling the air around her.

From: Waltwonders89@gmail.com
To: Jocasta.franklin@49agency.co.uk
Date: 29 April 2019, 21:22

Subject: Meeting

Hi Jocasta,

I know you must be incredibly busy, but I felt I had to write to you. I found your email on your agency's website, so I'm hoping this reaches you confidentially.

I'm a current master's student on Sofie Muller's course, and I haven't been having the best time, to be honest. I looked up your agency's address and saw that you work near the university. Is there any chance we could meet for a coffee? I know this might sound strange, but I think you're the only person who can help.

Either way, I'd appreciate it if you didn't mention this to Sofie. Many thanks and all best,

Walt

Her colleague was smashing the keys on his laptop, which gave an air of great importance to whatever he was typing. She wondered if the boy had typed the email like that: full of pumped-up determination. It was the way young men always wrote. If a woman had emailed her at work asking to meet, it would be full of apologies. Jo was always doling out apologies, even where they weren't needed. Years of practice had taught her to meticulously delete them from her correspondence.

The lack of apologies made the email hard to ignore, though, and maybe it would help Sofie to meet him face to face. She sent him a line back with a date and a time, implying she had many other pressing things to get to in her life, and then she left it in her Drafts folder without hitting the 'send' button for half an hour.

Nothing he said would matter. Jo couldn't imagine gaining clarity from this person. Some things simply remained unclear and stayed that way forever. But still, it would be good to hear how this mess had started, at least from a new point of view.

She met the boy, Walt, in a small café by the river. He was tall and good-looking, a far cry from the hapless, literary type she'd imagined, who had nothing better to do than troll Sofie. He looked nervous, which made her take him more seriously, because you don't write emails like that to strangers unless you're either a scammer or at your wits' end.

She waved, and when he came over she shook his hand. He seemed jittery, a vein bulging at his temple. She felt so sorry for him that she bought two slabs of shortbread and insisted he eat one, as though he was an elderly convalescent.

They sat in the corner of the café and she looked at him properly, taking in his neat hair and ironed shirt in an unusual shade of blue. She complimented it and he smiled for the first time.

'Once a stranger stopped me on the street to ask where I bought it. When I couldn't remember – it was an independent shop somewhere – the guy grabbed my collar and pulled it back to expose the label. I was so shocked, I just stood there and let him do it. And then he walked off as though nothing had happened. I guess I knew it was a good shirt after that.'

She was relieved that he didn't find it difficult to make small talk.

'Whatever the email you sent me was about,' she said, 'it took courage to reach out and ask for help.' If she was kind, would he go away?

'I didn't know what to do,' he replied. 'And I'm so grateful you could meet me. I really appreciate it.'

She sensed he'd gone to a good school. Maybe his mother also taught him how to speak politely, and he practised on her friends. Of course, it helped that he was pleasant-looking and likely knew it. You could forgive a lot because of a handsome, friendly face. Used in the right way, it was a weapon.

'I haven't yet mentioned anything to Sofie, like you asked,' she said. 'We're not married any more but she's still my friend, you know. I don't normally get involved with goings-on at the university, but after everything that's happened, I thought I might be able to help.'

He nodded. She could tell he wasn't really listening to her.

'It will sound ridiculous if I just spit it all out,' he said. Instead, he opened up his phone and handed it to her. On the screen was a chain of emails. 'It might just be easier if you read them.'

Like anyone with half a brain, the first thing she did was tap on the email address to check it was genuine. But weren't there ways nowadays to get around that, make it look real? He looked like he might know how to do that sort of thing.

'It's cold and lonely in this house in winter. I need a strong man to help me bring in the logs and light the fire. Or you could keep me warm under a blanket . . .'

'. . . sometimes when I'm bored I'll think about that freckle above your lip. I can meditate on it endlessly . . . you've been given the gift of prettiness and while I get to look upon it, it's never wasted . . .'

'. . . I get these headaches sometimes, raging things just before bed. If you were here, I know you'd stroke me and make it better . . .'

Jo put the phone back on the table.

'Okay.' She felt oddly as though she were the one who'd been caught. 'This does read as quite an inappropriate relationship.'

She wanted to tell him that Sofie had been known to get close to students and write compromising messages. It was part of her shtick, like a dog who just couldn't help sticking its nose into people's crotches. And his replies held the same promise of intimacy.

'You say in your replies that you couldn't wait to see her again?' she said. 'To look after her? To cover her with kisses head to toe?'

He sighed.

'I didn't know what the hell to do. She promised me she'd get me published.'

All this for another book that no one would ever read, thought Jo.

'It looks bad,' she said. She felt she could admit that. 'But it looks pretty bad on you too. You should think before going public with it.'

He nodded slowly, retrieving his phone.

'I thought you'd have questions for me, like how long it went on for or how it ended or why she'd write such things. Why don't you? Is it because it happens a lot?'

She felt tired. She had thought, coming here, that he might have some answers, but it was only more questions.

'I was married to Sofie for five years,' she told him. 'Then I left. I wish I could help, but what would I know about what she does or doesn't do with her students?'

'She's still your friend, isn't she? And *you* were her student.'

'A hundred years ago.'

'She's your friend *now*.'

Jo shook her head, looking for the mole above his lip. Ah, there it was. Where was his mother? Why had he come to her?

'I know you won't like this, but I want to give you a piece of advice I wish someone had once given me.'

He waited obediently for what she was going to say, like the schoolboy he still was.

'Sometimes,' she said, 'life is about finding out that the thing you thought you were good at, maybe isn't the thing you should pursue. There isn't one path. If something's not working, or you weren't as talented as you thought, sometimes it's okay to quit and look for something else. There's no shame in quitting.' It felt right. It was like Sofie always said: you just had to deliver the lesson with confidence. It wasn't your job to believe it.

'You think I'm saying all this because she told me I wasn't a good writer?'

'I don't know what she told you.'

He sat back into his chair, suddenly relaxed, his face a golden glow of epiphany.

'I think you believe me, that's what I think.'

'It doesn't matter either way.' She had to stop this now, before it went any further.

He cocked his head up, a half-smile.

'It does, actually. It means other people who know her might believe me, too. Might recognise her writing style and the way she acts with her students. Might put it together as part of a pattern.'

'Or they might think you're jumping on a bandwagon of allegations.'

'Why would I give a shit if she stole someone's half-baked short story? She took over my life and then hung me out to dry.'

She wanted to say the way he could get his life back was by walking out the door and leaving this part of it behind.

Instead she said, 'You seem like a nice man—'

'You seem like a bit of a bitch, actually,' he shot back, interrupting her.

She couldn't help laughing, because the way he said it was funny.

It took the sting out of the moment. It wasn't so bad, all of this. Tomorrow, she might wake up and warm her milk, slowly, in a pan, pour herself a cup of coffee and not think about any of this. But she could tell he wasn't done.

'At first,' he said, 'she just demanded my attention. She sent me lots of messages in between classes, and I didn't mind. Then, she wanted me to come over. Shave her legs, cut her toenails. I put the clippings in a jar by the side of her bed.' He grimaced, and Jo felt a shiver of recognition. 'Then, I had to get under the covers, hold her. Let her . . . stroke me. There was always lots of booze. And books everywhere, so it was hard to forget how powerful she was. Look, I grew up with money. Do I give a shit about a designer bag? But it was all sort of part of this picture she created. It gets to you, even if you don't think it does. Once, she told me I was young enough to be her child. The last straw was when I woke up and she was on top of me, just like that.'

'No,' said Jo. The word came out sounding empty. She didn't want to – couldn't – believe it.

'There are petitions online and campaigns about sexual harassment and assaults at universities, mostly run by women, of course,' Walt said. 'So, the evidence is there that as institutions they don't take allegations against their students and their employees seriously.' He cracked a piece of shortbread in half, but didn't eat it. 'And of course, it makes sense that they wouldn't want to take allegations against Sofie Muller seriously, because of who she is and the kind of revenue she brings in. She's worth a lot. She has a clear monetary value that's worth a lot more than us. But I've lived it.'

He was nodding as he spoke, and afterwards Jo would find it hard to forget; the way he nodded along to what he said, as though he was the only one who would.

'If you ever wondered if universities give a shit about rape,' he said, 'I can tell you first-hand: they don't.'

Two

Alice

Along with some guest tutors, Robert took over the rest of our classes. In the first workshop after we heard the news, he stood at the front of the room like he was trying to boost morale at the start of a war and told us not to worry about our studies, which shouldn't be affected too much. The whole department was hopeful she'd be back in post soon. If not, they'd find a replacement as soon as possible.

He looked pleased with himself, as though Sofie had just been shot in the head and he was being sworn in. We all sat around, dumbstruck. By that point, we'd exchanged countless texts and emails with each other, but no one seemed sure whether anything we'd read was true. We invited each other into a safe space: if anyone has experienced anything, they could talk about it.

No one said a word except to share various links to Reddit and Twitter threads about the accusations. Were they credible? In smaller groups, there was one name that hung in the air like drizzle, faint but unavoidable: Walt.

Even Robert himself pointed out there was one student who was noticeably absent from class, and we should take that to mean what we will.

'That doesn't mean he's the one who's done anything wrong,'

Grace said. I looked around. Everyone was staring at her in silence. Robert pressed his lips together in a smile. 'If you're implying it's a sign of guilt, I don't think that's fair, that's all.'

'I'd be careful about what you decide is and isn't fair, Grace.' He said her name as though it was alleged. We were all temporary here, passing through the chaos.

Grace snorted beside me.

'What is *that* supposed to mean?' She was tying her hair into a French plait with casual dexterity.

The movement seemed to bother Robert, who said, 'Are you quite finished?'

'I need something to do with my hands while I listen to the details of the unfortunate persecution of Sofie Muller,' she said. 'Please, continue.'

He slapped down a pile of handouts, told us to take one and pass them on and asked Grace to start reading aloud. It was an extract from a debut novel, which Sofie had been intending to share with us as an example of a strong voice.

'I'd rather not, if that's okay. I have a sore throat.'

Robert looked like he'd been pelted with something unpleasant and was stoically resisting the urge to wipe it from his face.

'I know this is hard for everyone, but it's better if we just rally together.' He clapped his hands. 'The show must go on.'

Grace undid the plait she had just created and fluffed her hair over her shoulders. 'It's not that,' she said, without looking up at him. 'I think some of us find it hard to actually concentrate on what we're reading if we have to read it out loud, like we're at school.'

'I'm just following Sofie's lesson plan,' said Robert. 'Would you like to come up and teach the class?'

'No, but I'd like you to talk to us as though we're adults, which, by the way, we are.'

He folded his arms across his chest.

'I can tell all of this is getting to you. That's understandable, but it's in your best interests to carry on. I'm sure that before we know it, Sofie will be back.'

'Fantastic,' Grace said. She opened her mouth to continue, but Henderson started speaking, reading out the passage as though nothing had happened. Grace shot him a look, but he carried on.

When the excerpt was finished, Robert thanked Henderson and asked us what we thought of the passage. No one said anything. We were all in our own worlds, but this time it wasn't a world of fiction. We hadn't listened to a word Henderson had said.

After the class, I followed Grace to the Students' Union and queued behind her. She ordered a ham and cheese panini and I did the same. While the students behind the bar heated them in the hot metal press, I joined her at the end of the counter. She hadn't noticed me there.

'Oh, hi,' she said flatly.

'I admired the way you handled Robert in class,' I told her. 'Everything is just so weird right now.'

'I couldn't stand how smug he was about it, that's all. The way he was following her instructions like he was Prince Regent.'

I smiled. 'Do you think she's coming back?'

'Of course. Does anyone think she isn't?'

'So, you think she didn't do it then?' All her little emails with book recommendations and witticisms had ceased the moment she was suspended. In that strange period, I sometimes felt as though I'd imagined her.

Grace watched a student slipping our sandwiches into paper bags using metal tongs.

'I didn't say that.'

We each took our lunch and Grace gestured towards a plastic table where we could eat.

'If you're asking me if I think she's a thief or a liar or an abuser, then it stands to reason that she's probably all of those things.' She took a bite out of her panini, the cheese pulling a hot, stretchy trail from the bread to her mouth, and blew a breath out hastily, fanning a hand to warn me it was still hot.

I opened my own bag with caution.

'But how can you be so sure?'

She swallowed and gasped for air.

'I'm not sure. But I believe Walt. Even if all he did about it was write those stupid Reddit posts.'

This was news to me.

'He did? He wrote them *all*?'

'Well, the ones that started off the trend. I asked him and he admitted it.'

'But why would he do that?'

'Because of what she did, I guess. What else was he meant to do? I thought he told you about it anyway.'

'He did tell me.' I peeled off a corner of bread and put it in my mouth. 'I just didn't hear it.'

'You're not alone, you know, in thinking he made it up.'

I thought about the whole class exchanging incredulous messages.

'I believe him now,' I told her, 'but I guess it's too late to gain back his trust. How come you believed him immediately?'

She exhaled derisively. 'We've all met Sofie. Would it surprise you about any of them? Would it surprise you about Robert? The question you should be asking is why *wouldn't* I believe him.'

Judging it safe, I finally bit into my sandwich. The cheese was rich and tangy and the ham was pleasantly synthetic, like a child's snack. This was why we weren't really friends, I realised, because when it came down to it, she thought I was weak. She thought I couldn't see through them.

I swallowed and said, 'Can I ask you something?'

'Sure,' she said.

'I always thought he might have tried it on with you. You don't have to tell me. But I wanted to know if he did.'

'Didn't he try it on with everyone? We only kissed, that's all.'

I dropped the rest of my sandwich on the table.

'Oh God. When? Is that why you're always so scathing to him in his classes?'

'Wait, did you mean Robert?' She laughed, slamming a hand down on the table. 'I'd cut off his balls if he ever came within two feet of me. He wouldn't dare.' She grimaced. 'God, no.'

I looked at the stringy cheese of my sandwich, congealing and going cold.

'Who are you talking about then?' I said, though I thought I knew the answer.

She shrugged.

'Isn't it like a rite of passage? Walt. I'm talking about Walt.'

Molly pulled me into her office. It was the same office I always worked in at the back of the industrial unit, but when she was there it felt like hers alone. She was wearing athletic gear, busy on her phone and laptop planning the next workout with her PR contact.

'I came in specially to talk to you,' she said. 'Alice, are you aware that deliveries are often arriving late, or not being processed as efficiently as they could be?'

She hovered over where I was sitting beside her desk, as though she might leave at any moment. In the email inviting me to come in on my day off, she'd promised me lunch. It was mid-afternoon and my stomach was gurgling. There was, of course, no lunch.

'I shouldn't have to tell you that it's not Olena's job to do what she did,' Molly said.

She liked to tell me that before I joined, she was in the kitchen herself working the machines, working her ass off. All I'd seen her do was send emails, which I wanted to point out didn't count.

'It was my fault,' I admitted, putting my hands in my lap deferentially. I hated the way Molly's hair was always thick and shiny.

She paced around, and I imagined in her mind she was scrolling through the chapters of the one management book she'd read for her MBA.

'I just . . . don't get it,' she said finally.

'That evening everything was running late, and Olena wanted to stay anyway. She offered to help pack the last orders and I let her. It was a mistake.' I tucked my hair behind my ears and looked up at her. I knew I didn't sound very convincing. I thought about standing up, but then I wouldn't know what to do with my hands. 'I don't know what happened, I can't believe Olena did anything wrong.'

'But the reason you don't know is that you weren't here when you should have been.' She crossed her arms. 'Even if it's midnight, it's your job. That's what I've entrusted to you.'

Sometimes I thought about the night the label gun for the expiry dates stopped working and I spent an hour writing them all by hand. I'd called Molly to ask what to do and she'd sounded genuinely concerned that I might be having a breakdown. It was a stupid, easy job and I felt stupid doing it.

'It's just . . . *juice*,' I said, because I had nothing else to say.

'*Just juice?*' she repeated, incredulous. 'It's my *business*. It's everyone's livelihoods.' She gestured towards the women in the kitchen. It was true, I thought – it was her business, but they were the ones doing all the work. 'If you don't think it's important, you can leave whenever you want.'

I wondered in what world cold-pressed juice should feel this important. Did she know that while the world was dying and millions of people lived in food poverty, she'd built a business that threw away hundreds of bin bags of vegetable pulp a week? Most of the time I didn't think about climate change or injustice, but she *definitely* never thought about it.

'You won't fire Olena, will you?' I said.

Molly's expression softened. It was clear that Olena was her favourite. And why wouldn't she be?

'Of course not,' she said impatiently. 'She works harder than anyone.'

When I didn't say anything, it seemed to confirm her decision.

'It's clear that you've been too distracted by other work,' she said, 'and things aren't getting done properly. You're falling behind, becoming negligent. I think it's best for everyone if you finish up the day's orders and then head home. I will make sure to give you this week's wages.'

'And will you reimburse me for the business expenses I recently had to put on my credit card?' I asked her.

She shrugged.

'I haven't been working today,' I pointed out, 'so there's nothing for me to "finish up".'

'Fine,' she said. 'That works out well, then.'

It was only later that I realised she was trying to tell me that I'd been nothing but a pain, and now she finally had a reason to be rid of me.

'Thanks for everything, all the same,' I said. It was the worst job I'd ever had, but being asked to leave felt humiliating. Now Molly could tell herself she'd won.

After she jumped in an Uber to run to a barre class, I packed up what was left of my things. Olena came to say goodbye and to tell me I was better off. She held out a notebook.

'You left it last time you were here,' she said. 'I had a little look. I wanted to know the things you wrote about.'

I swallowed, reaching for it, pressing the pages between my fingers. Inside were scenes from my work in progress, all about her.

'I couldn't tell if the story was any good, but I like the way you write. Oh, don't turn red like the beetroot, I only looked at a couple of pages.'

I sighed, relieved.

'Okay,' I said. 'That's okay.'

'It was about me, wasn't it?' Seeing my expression, she added: 'I don't mind, Alice.'

'Some of it was inspired by the things you said, I suppose. But it's just made up, mostly,' I told her. 'I hope you're not offended.'

'Actually, it's flattering,' she said, grinning. 'It's nice to think you cared about me, this place, enough to want to write about it. All this time I thought you were off in your own world when you left here, but in a way you were always thinking about me.'

They said it was better, didn't they, to beg forgiveness than ask permission? But Olena made me feel as though I didn't need to do either.

'It all feels so stupid now, the writing. I'm thinking about stopping.'

Olena shook her head.

'You just have to keep going, Alice, or you'll end up like me. The time just passes whether you're doing what you want to do or not. So it's better to keep doing it.'

'Did you really not mind me writing about you?' I said. I couldn't quite believe it.

'Not so much. Maybe there was a bit of me in there, but it sounds like you. It's all so *Alice*. Anyway, you had to write about something.'

It was true that even with an imagined character, it was hard to get away from yourself.

'I will be sorry to leave you,' I told her. 'You were the only good thing about this place.' I cradled the notebook against my chest, wishing I could burn it.

'I am sad, too. But don't worry about work, about Molly,' she said. 'She's kind of a bitch.'

This made me feel better, and I let out a quavering laugh.

'She used you, that's all,' she continued. 'If you feel bad about anything, remember that it's her, not you. *She* used *you*.'

* * *

Later that night, Hassan from the delivery company called me and I had to tell him I wouldn't be their point of contact any more.

'I've left the business,' I said, as though I'd ever been a part of it.

'I'm sorry to hear that,' he said gravely. 'In that case, could you maybe pass on a message? We found a bag of juices in the back of one of the vans that was meant to be part of a delivery last week. Did you guys know it was missing?'

He sounded so apologetic that I fumbled my words, eventually managing to say, 'Just throw the bag away if it's already out of date.'

It turned out I was fired for nothing, but I was glad, because now I was free to write.

Three

Jo

She'd never forget the day she left Sofie. She walked miles to the train station and caught the 7.38 into town. She'd set up a flat there, ahead of time, so she couldn't back out.

Jo used to like reading books that Sofie had disparaged, curled up on the sofa as she flipped through novels Sofie described as 'all marketing, no merit'. It enraged Sofie, so Jo kept doing it. Now, she could look back and see how awful she herself had been, trying to bait Sofie at every opportunity and get her to say something so appalling that she would have no choice but to leave.

'Those books are trash,' Sofie said, 'which means your brain is trash.' She wanted Jo to workshop a new novel with her, the way they'd always done it, and had brought home sheafs of students' work. 'Let's sit on the living-room floor and go through the best ones. I already have an idea for a story that could really sell. I told the student it wasn't literary enough for the course, and she should use another idea for her work in progress. But actually, it was the best thing I've read in months. Not so much the writing, which could be much improved, but the story. The story just works.'

Sofie had already thought of ways they could tweak it to make it different enough. It was like borrowing a melody from a song that got stuck in your head.

The process of putting it on paper was, however, always more sophisticated. It was like surgery, taking out what was necessary and transplanting it into something entirely new. Sometimes, Sofie had watched over Jo's shoulder while she did it, mapping the new story out on index cards and scattering them on the living room floor. She didn't watch Jo when she wrote, though. That was quiet and solitary and Sofie wasn't a creator, not really. She was a butcher. Her work came in when the whole thing needed a knife. Eventually, it would be impossible to tell that it had ever been anything else. It was distinctly theirs. In the end, distinctly Sofie's.

After doing it for almost a decade, Jo had grown tired. It was Sofie's show, she would say to herself while she was washing up with murky water leaking into her Marigolds. While she was wiping the dust from the skirting boards with an old cloth – the bits the cleaner had missed – she realised she'd grown tired of being a secondary character in someone else's story.

Sometimes, the thoughts would consume her and she'd sit on the sofa, staring at nothing. It was easy to forget that sitting and contemplating was actually hard-wired into our DNA, and we'd created distractions to rid ourselves of this essential ritual. The novels were one of the distractions. They felt useless.

Sofie would happen upon her and sigh, saying Jo was having a 'Jocasta Day'. She always called it that, as if Jo was sick, but in a way peculiar to her: as if she'd done it to herself.

It was on one of these days that Jo got an email from a friend about a job in marketing. At first it seemed absurd. She was a writer! Then she realised the subtext. Her unhappiness was clearly oozing out of her, and her friend wanted to help. It was easy to think unhappy marriages were normal and therefore invisible, but they were clearly discernible to other people. It was like a smell, and when you lived in it, you didn't notice it any more, but others were hit with it like a wall. They usually pretended they hadn't noticed anything, but this email was a clear attempt at rescue.

Then, like it had been perfectly written into the story of their marriage, Sofie took one of the 'trashy' books that Jo loved and ripped all the pages out. Not in a rage, either, but one by one. With care. Then she left them in an orderly pile on the floor as though to prove her point.

Jo didn't give her the reaction she wanted, this time, and Sofie must have realised she was losing her. The key was to keep your audience captive long enough to allow you to behave badly. If you took it too far, you had to give them a little respite, a little comic or romantic relief.

Jo had already packed her suitcase to move out when Sofie suggested a mini-break together.

'We can go to the South of France and drink overpriced wine, and write the new novel,' she said. She must have seen reluctance in Jo's expression, because she hastily continued, 'Or not! – either way the novel doesn't matter, because I love you.'

It hadn't been said for a while and that made it even more special, didn't it? For a moment, all was well. After they made love that night, the last thing Sofie said to her before she drifted off to sleep was:

'I'd be nothing without you.'

Jo heard it in her dream, could picture Sofie saying it next to azure water, the waves crashing against French rocks. In the end it was just another of Sofie's mantras, she thought when she woke at 3 a.m. People always said the same things, over and over. Trying to change anyone was pointless.

She had sneaked out early and grabbed the suitcase she'd hidden downstairs. It was easy to imagine that Sofie would, if anything, gain more momentum without her. Sofie could be with anyone, and she'd still be perfectly herself. How could she say she'd be nothing without Jo? Jo didn't believe it.

But that was then. Almost ten years had passed, and she believed it now.

Sofie invited Jo over for a swim. The weather was becoming hotter as late spring arrived. It was the kind of time the students were usually invited over, but this year, Sofie was alone. Maybe she'd never have students around to her house ever again. The thought was a relief to Jo, but she put it to the back of her mind while she shifted gears in her old Volkswagen.

When she arrived, Sofie seemed sullen but alert and the house was very clean. Sofie started to tell Jo about the different journalists who'd been calling – she could listen to the voicemails if she liked – and how obnoxious the press was.

'They just want to fill their papers with something people can gawk at, and there's a new story every week about someone in a prominent position misbehaving.'

Jo was about to say that just because Sofie didn't deserve this – didn't she? – others still might.

But then Sofie said: 'Of course, the stories are mostly about men. The best and easiest way to discredit a woman is to say that her talent isn't real, it's stolen. That she doesn't deserve what she's got, because she could never be smart enough to actually get it herself.'

This was difficult to deny, because it was true. Jo kept her counsel, and Sofie continued, 'As soon as there's any whiff of a scandal, a woman's sexual history is brought up to be used against her. Even when it's completely irrelevant.'

This was true, too.

Sofie was wearing a swimming costume, a sarong tied in a loose knot at her waist. She would have looked beautiful and elegant, if she wasn't so angry.

'Has there even been *one* credible or official accusation against me of a sexual nature?' she railed. 'Of course not. The little shits aren't even brave enough to make something up.'

Now Jo felt she had to say something.

'But there are plenty of accusations, online. They just don't have real names attached to them.'

'And what's an accusation without a name? Without a person behind it? It's an IP address. A block of type on a screen. It's nothing.'

Jo was impressed Sofie knew what an IP address was.

Sofie said, 'I've been told the plagiarism case won't go any further, after the lawyers ascertained there wasn't enough evidence to prosecute. They're going to try and trace the IP address from the Reddit threads, to figure out who it was. I should be back in my post before the month is out.'

It was extraordinary, Jo thought, the lengths people went to, to start something and then simply drop it. She was relieved: her own name had only appeared in the article as a potential victim of Sofie's, a claim so absurd it was easy to rebuff.

'You could've called and told me this on the phone,' she said.

Sofie flicked her hair over her shoulder, the loose waves falling over her face.

'I thought it was better to tell you in person. To celebrate.'

'It actually hasn't occurred to you that this affects me too, has it? That it has the potential to implicate me?'

Jo had woken up the night before to go to the loo, her hand fumbling for the light switch outside the bathroom. When she flicked it on, she had a thought: if Sofie goes down, am I going with her? She couldn't get back to sleep after that.

Sofie held her arms out.

'Jocasta, if you came here to deliver another lecture, I'm really not in the mood.'

There was a serving fork left out on the side from Sofie's last meal, an unusual oversight. Jo wanted to pick it up and stab her with it.

Sofie turned and opened the fridge. She worried some bottles inside and asked Jo if she wanted a cordial or something stronger.

'Do you still keep your toenails after you cut them?' Jo asked her. Sofie laughed.

'I know you always hated that. My little collection of clippings.'

Jo had asked Sofie about it before. They disgusted her, curled together in a jar. Why did Sofie bother keeping them? Sofie had replied that you had to be careful. It was the kind of thing your enemies could find and use against you. Until then, Jo had never pegged her as the superstitious type. Now, however, she understood – there must be plenty of people who'd like to make a Voodoo doll of Sofie.

'Did you do it? Did you touch them?' Out it came.

Sofie stopped rummaging, her head still in the fridge. She turned round, holding a bottle of rosé, and half-smiled.

'Did I touch what?'

'*Them*. Your students. Have you ever touched your students?'

'Well.' Sofie pulled open a drawer and retrieved a corkscrew. 'I've touched you. Does that count?'

'Walt? Did you touch Walt?'

Sofie dropped the corkscrew, which clattered loudly against the marble work surface.

'How do you know his name?' she said. Her face was white and tense.

'Just answer the question.'

'How do you know his name?'

'So . . . you did then, you did touch him?'

In response, Sofie picked up the bottle of wine and screamed as she smashed it down on the cold ceramic floor of the sink:

'He was just a little boy who was angry that he had no talent!'

Shards of glass and drops of wine flew up and Jo leapt back, her heart thumping in the hollow of her throat, then froze, worried that if she moved again Sofie would come at her.

'Sofie,' she said softly. 'I had to ask. It's one of those things. I had to ask, just once.'

Sofie shook her head. Her fingers were wet and a fragment of glass was stuck to one cheek.

'My life is over, so you can ask me anything you want. But you can't expect me to react well when you do.'

'What about the girl? Did you touch that girl?' A lump was caught in Jo's throat, as if she was trying to swallow the words. 'Alice.'

Sofie's eyes filled with tears, staring at the broken bottle. She didn't reply.

Jo raised her voice.

'She was here when I came over that time. She was wearing your clothes. You didn't touch her, did you? It's all right. If you just say you didn't, we can both get on with our lives.'

'The day you left,' said Sofie, after a brief silence, 'I thought you were the worst person in the world. But you were just acting on instinct, like a dog. It wasn't brave to leave. It was cowardly.' She sighed heavily. 'No Jocasta, I didn't touch her. Are you happy now?'

Could Jo be happy being the coward? Jo had been the one to leave her, all those years ago, but Sofie had drawn her back in. Had she done that just to prove that Jo would always come? Because she could control her, or because she loved her?

'None of this makes me happy,' Jo said. It was hard to admit that her happiest days were seemingly behind her: sitting on the floor with Sofie, writing, plotting, reading aloud to each other, living in their own little world. There had once been a point to all this, a craft to it, before the outside world came in.

Sofie drew a hand across her face and started to wipe the shards of glass from the counter into the sink with a tea towel.

'All we have is each other now. Maybe it's all we ever had,' she said.

What had they done in the years spent apart? It was hard to tell sometimes. Maybe they were both getting older, losing their grip.

'You know I believe you,' Jo said. 'I have to believe you.' Or else – what?

Sofie looked up at her, with the kind of smile that made the hair on Jo's arms stand up to some invisible force, some shift in energy and matter. If Jo looked hard enough, maybe she could see the universe rearranging itself, the particles realigning between them. Maybe she could feel the glow from infinitesimal golden orbs swirling as Sofie moved to kiss her. Jo relented to the sweet press of lips, and felt her body relax from the tonic.

'The thing is, sweet Jocasta of mine, we can win them all back, can't we?' Sofie crooned, stroking her hair reassuringly. 'Everyone loves an underdog. What better time to come out with a new piece of work?'

Perhaps Sofie was right: there was no better time. Who wouldn't want to read the latest novel from newsworthy Sofie, after almost a decade of silence?

'But we'd talked about my own writing, my own novel,' she said.

'Yes, yes, of course, of course.' Sofie was still running her hand across Jo's hair. 'Of course we'll get to that. But first, I have an idea that needs your help.'

It was all about the work, wasn't it? Getting lost in the process of mapping out, cutting, creating, the kind of thing that was as good for your heart as a marathon. The rest of Jo's life was simply noise, a distraction. It didn't matter how the work began, all that mattered was what they were working towards.

What did bravery matter when you had choices you could exercise? Why did something have to be brave to be good? Sometimes things just had to be done. Now, more than ever, was the time to get on and do them.

Sofie fetched her laptop and opened it up, sliding it in front of Jo. The blue light from the screen enveloped Jo's face as she began to read. Sofie put a hand on Jo's knee and squeezed. Jo smiled.

Four

Alice

I hadn't talked to Walt for a few weeks, so when he texted and asked me to meet him to help with a plan he had, I felt a hit of relief.

We met outside the main building. On the ground floor were rows of lecture halls and seminar rooms, and below ground were the faculty's offices.

At first, he was gracious.

'How's your novel?'

He crossed his arms and leaned against the red brick of the building as though we were waiting for someone else.

'It's hanging in there. And yours?'

'I've finally finished a draft.' He was holding a manuscript under his arm. 'I just came from the library – I may finally have something I'd be happy to hand in at the end of the year.'

'Can I read it?'

He shook his head. 'I had to do something after spending too much time "complaining" and not enough time writing.'

'Who said that?' I asked.

'The Vice Provost. He's been pretty quick to dismiss me. He told me that if I put my name to an official grievance, there would be an internal investigation. But I fucked up with the Reddit posts. At the time I was so lost, it seemed like the only thing I could do. Even though everything I said was true, because I used multiple usernames and a load of other accounts then chimed in, it makes it look like it was all me, like I just made shit up.'

'So, you did write them, then?'

'Quite a few. It wasn't like I could sign them: "Kind regards, Walt." But they weren't all me. The VP must know the deluge that's come in since has nothing to do with me.'

'But it looks like you created a bunch of sock puppet accounts.'

'Instead of what it should look like, which is that *she's* really fucking guilty.' He sighed. 'The VP said that without sufficient third-party evidence, there's no way to prove what had happened. Basically, unless there was someone around to watch her fuck me, it didn't happen.'

I wondered if they'd have been more likely to believe a woman.

'In a way I think she's clever. She won't have gone around trying to sleep with the whole cohort,' I said – my way of saying he was on his own. I couldn't tell him what had happened to me. 'I do want to help,' I added, weakly.

'They said if I leave quietly, they won't name me,' he said. 'They'll still give me a good reference, and I can get my degree remotely if I finish my dissertation. In a few months, the course will be over anyway. I can get it all back, except the months and the days and the hours.'

I wondered if the fact that he was talking to me without anger meant that he had forgiven me.

All I said was: 'Are we going inside?'

He stood to attention as if I'd pulled him out of a dream. We went in and took the stairs to the lower ground floor. We'd all been to Sofie's office before, and we knew that after six o'clock it would be locked. She hadn't been in the building for weeks anyway, but it felt safer to go out of hours.

As we stood outside the closed door, gathering courage, I studied the posters of novels from the course hung along the corridor.

Walt took a hammer out of his inside pocket.

'I got it from the DIY shop in town.' He passed it from hand to hand, weighing it in his palms. 'In Singapore, you can get caned as a punishment for robbery.' He looked at me. 'And rape.'

I took the hammer from him.

'You're not getting cold feet, are you?' I said.

'Caning sounds so primitive, doesn't it? It's a hangover from colonialism.'

I grimaced. He beckoned for the hammer, and I handed it back. Then, without warning, he squeezed the claw end between the door and its frame and kicked at the same time. He hit the door handle with the blunt end three times, kicked again, and the door flew open. The noise seemed preposterously loud, and I felt sure a security guard was about to come running; I looked up the stairs where we'd come from, but there really was no one around.

The room was neat and orderly, just as I had last seen it. Walt pushed the door closed behind us, with only a few splinters littering the carpet. I thought once we were inside I'd know what to look for, know where I could find the answer. Walt wanted compromising information, and I felt like I owed it to him to help.

We went through her drawers and searched around her desk. We found scraps of notes, mostly indecipherable. On her pinboard, I spotted a note from her ex-wife. It transcribed a love poem and told Sofie to enjoy the mug, to carry the writer with her wherever she went. 'So you'll never be without me,' it read, 'all my love, your darling Jo.' I wondered if she kept it there for the sake of her students and their intrigue around her ceramic figure mug. Or maybe it simply mattered to her.

There were notebooks that were mostly empty, cuttings from newspapers and stacks of unfinished university paperwork. While I kept looking, Walt tried to get into her computer. He tried various passwords – 'password1', as used by most older people, then the names of each of her novels – but none of them worked. I must have watched too many action movies, as I half expected him to pull out a piece of software that would hack into the system, but as I crouched beside a filing cabinet whose individually lockable drawers were mercifully unlocked, I looked up and saw a man fumbling his way around a keyboard. This wasn't a sophisticated operation.

I was starting to panic. Not about being caught, but about failing to find anything. The last drawer in the cabinet was locked.

'Shit,' I said.

'No luck?'

'No. You?'

He wheeled back in his chair, slammed his hands on the desk. 'Pointless.' Then he came over and went through the drawers I'd already been through, as though he was checking my work. I was still sitting on the floor next to the cabinet. 'I guess, why would she keep anything of importance here?' He pulled at the last drawer. 'No key for this one?'

'No key.'

'It was worth a try.'

He went back to the computer again and I clambered up from the floor, deflated. I spotted his manuscript where he'd put it on the corner of the desk, and quietly took it and read the first few pages. What I saw surprised me, but before I could say anything he let out a grunt of aggravation at the screen, then looked over at me and saw what I was reading.

'Only a crazy person would agree to do all this,' he said. 'I'm sorry about what I said the last time we spoke.'

'Ugh, don't,' I said. 'You sound like you're saying goodbye to me at a train station in a black-and-white movie.' I handed him back the manuscript. 'What happened to the woman murdered in the woods?'

He shrugged.

'This one's a love story,' I said. 'You're writing a love story.' What I didn't say was that it was some of the most beautiful writing I'd read in a long time, and I wished it was about me.

He opened his mouth and closed it. Paused. Then: 'You know we can't be together, don't you, Alice? You didn't believe me. We can't recover from that.'

'Okay, I know. I know that now.' Someone could come in at any moment, so I should say everything I wanted to say. 'But Walt . . . I do care about you. So much.'

'You didn't believe me at all, did you?' There was something sad and inevitable about the way he said it. 'I've scrambled around this entire year, trying to get people on my side. Because I was totally exposed and no one believed a word of it. There's nothing like people thinking you're a phony.'

'I'm sorry.' I had imagined this conversation over and over again. But now we were having it, I felt worse. 'Did you kiss Grace?' I said. 'Before you kissed me, did you kiss her?'

'*She* listened to me. *She* believed me.'

I deserved that.

It felt like a secret, how much I loved him, and how much I would continue to love him after he left the room. It would hang over me, I imagined, for months, possibly years. I'd have to get used to it until it became invisible but ever-present, like the sound of the railway from an open window.

'No,' I said. 'In answer to your question, at the time, I couldn't believe you. Not at all.'

He smiled. Sometimes it was good to have the answer you wanted. It was satisfying when everyone stopped lying. I was happy for him.

'Ah,' he said. 'I do understand that. But I can't get past it.'

There are so many ways to say goodbye but, that day, he only had one. He gathered up his things and told me:

'It's okay, really. We'll see each other again soon.' That was a lie. 'I've always liked you so much, Alice.' That wasn't, but it only made things worse.

I watched him walk out of the broken door, my mind a blank, then looked helplessly around the office at the mess we had left behind.

On the desk was a pencil case I'd fished out of the desk drawer. It struck me that this was the kind of place you might keep something small that you didn't want to lose. I unzipped it, my heart racing, and hidden under a collection of the high-end HB pencils Sofie always used I found a small key. I tried it in the bottom drawer, which clicked open with a soft release to reveal one large notebook and a bundle of letters. I went through them hurriedly: thank-yous from students and other handwritten cards. At first, I couldn't work out what the notebook was for. I flipped through the heavily biro-indented pages, which turned with a satisfying crunch. Some of the handwriting was clearly Sofie's, but most of it I didn't recognise. I did, however, recognise the words. Everyone had read the article about Sofie by now. Everyone had flicked through the novels that supposedly borrowed extracts from students' writings. As I read, I realised that this notebook held the beginnings of one of these very stories. Plot points, notes, and even, slipped in a pocket at the back, the original extract from a student, with Sofie's own handwriting in the margins, telling them it could be better.

It was a thorough and comprehensive lift and shift. Anyone could see how blatantly Sofie had stolen from it. But looking at the sloping 'S' and looping 'J', I knew it wasn't Sofie's handwriting alone. Then – I remembered the handwritten note on Sofie's pinboard. *Your darling Jo.* It was the perfect match.

I slipped the notebook into my rucksack, locked the drawer and put the key back.

Five

On my way home, I noticed a missed call from my ex-boyfriend. We hadn't spoken in months. I decided to call him back as I walked towards halls.

He picked up immediately. 'Have you written a novel yet?'

'Some of it. I might scrap it and start again.' It felt good to talk to someone who had no vested interest in my writing. It felt good to declare I might delete every word.

'Can you do that?'

'That's the thing about novels. You can do whatever you want.'

He let out a small laugh, the kind that used to make me feel happy when I was hooked under his arm on a Sunday evening. The kind that was hard to say goodbye to, but I had. On reflection, everything about him seemed simple. I wondered why I always thought that was a bad thing.

'I might write about my predatory tutor.' I let it hang in the air. I could tell by the silence he didn't like the sound of that.

'What do you mean, Al? I hope he hasn't touched you?'

I didn't correct him. There was nothing to correct. If I said her name – *Sofie* – would it take the punch out of what happened?

'No, not really. Not at all, I mean,' I said.

'Oh. Good. I just wanted to see how you were,' he said. 'I thought maybe we could be friends.'

Did this mean there wasn't something wrong with me after all? Was I a good person? *Were* there good people?

'I haven't spoken to any of my real friends for months,' I said. 'This place is just a bubble. It makes stupid little things feel really important.'

'Is that your way of saying no?' He sounded hurt.

It was strange that with a little time and distance, the only thing that felt important in the end was the real world. If I said Sofie's name to him, it wouldn't mean anything. He wouldn't even recognise it.

'That's my way of saying yes,' I said.

Shortly after we broke into her office, Sofie was reinstated as the head of creative writing. The allegations against her were deemed to be unfounded and no official complaint of sexual harassment ever appeared. A think piece appeared online about the cult of taking down women in power. It referenced *The Times* article and the anonymous online posts about what it called Sofie's 'alleged misconduct', and took the view that this was part of a long history of sexual humiliation being used to silence women writers.

The piece was shared widely on social media and fitted neatly into the world like a key in a lock. It had been written with precision and was received in good faith: it spoke out against the suppression of women's writing. It called for creative liberation.

I had one last tutorial with Sofie before the summer began and my only task was to finish the portion of my novel that would become my dissertation. After weeks of not seeing her on campus, I wondered if she would appear cowed or somehow smaller, but as soon as she opened up her patched-up office door I could see this wasn't the case.

She looked as beautiful as ever in a powder-blue shift dress, her hair pulled away from her face.

'Alice, it's good to see you,' she said, without acknowledging her absence. I took her lead and didn't mention it. 'How's the girl who has the affair?' She sat down on her swivel chair and I glanced quickly at the filing cabinet where I'd crouched a matter of days before.

'Sorry, who?' I said.

'The one in your book.' She clicked on her computer screen so it lit up and rapidly typed a password. It was a marvel that such a small action lay between her entire online life and the rest of us.

'It's coming together.' I nodded firmly, trying to look convincing. Her expression was unreadable.

'If I'm being honest Alice, I don't think it's strong enough for publication.'

I sat down in the chair facing her desk, my heart sinking.

'But it's almost finished,' I said, surprised.

She sucked her teeth.

'If you're set on submitting it for your dissertation, I can't stop you. But beyond that, I wouldn't know what more we can do with it. I think it's unlikely to set the literary world alight.' She tilted her head to one side, and I felt horribly patronised by her faux sympathy. 'A woman having an affair is hardly a new idea. Even if it is a story about desire and consent.'

I knew what she was doing, leading me to abandon my work. She must've guessed I was part of the break-in. But seeing through it all didn't stop me from feeling crushed. 'I thought you liked the setting, the scenes at the juice kitchen?'

'Sure, that was unusual. But sometimes you have to ask yourself: who cares? Really, who gives a shit?'

As I gaped at her, lost for words, she turned back to her computer to pull up her timetable.

'There simply isn't enough time before the end of the year to try writing something new. You can defer for a year, or you can submit what you already have, which would just about pass muster.'

I felt the weight of my rucksack against my foot. I had been debating whether to say anything, but she had handed me the keys to her undoing.

'Actually, I have a new idea,' I said. 'I want to write about a student who accuses her professor of sexual assault.' Her eyes widened ever so slightly, and I continued. 'I've been thinking about it, and you might be right. The literary world might not be set alight by another tale of domestic woes. But it might like some confessional auto-fiction from a student of the notorious Sofie Muller.'

She remained composed. Her voice when she spoke was level and cold.

'You would do that?'

'It's been a hell of a year,' I said. I felt invincible, reckless. 'And aren't you the one always telling us to write what we know?'

She snorted, drumming her fingers on the desk. I couldn't work out if she was going to slap me or shake my hand.

'And you think people are going to take notice of something like that?' she said.

I nodded, holding her chilly blue gaze. 'Timing is everything.'

She stopped drumming, seemed to come to a decision.

'No one will believe it's anything other than fiction.'

'Maybe not,' I shot back. 'But you can't stop me.'

I reached down to my rucksack and pulled out her notebook, opening it up but keeping a tight grip on it.

'You won't call in any favours from friends,' I told her. 'You won't try and stop the novel from being published. If you do, I'll tell everyone what you did to me. What you did to Walt, too. And if all else fails, this notebook will certainly convince people of something.'

It was satisfying to have figured out her other secret, to feel the power of my knowledge hovering over her. I could carry it around inside me, a bell waiting to be rung.

She gazed at the notebook, which she clearly recognised. There were spots of hectic colour on her cheekbones. I had never seen her blush before. I hadn't quite imagined she could.

'Look at the handwriting,' she said eventually. 'That notebook isn't even mine.'

'I know,' I said. 'That's the whole point, isn't it? I know whose it is.'

I closed the notebook and put it in my rucksack.

She stood up, pushing her chair away from her so that it wheeled to the edge of her desk, and I flinched, still unsure whether she would attempt to wrestle the book away from me and risk losing her famous poise.

'It was you then?' She stood over me, her eyes darting, clearly calculating her next move. I could feel my lip trembling so I bit down on it, hard, and stood up to meet her.

'I'm sorry about your door.'

She couldn't help but smile at that, and I felt a twinge of triumph.

'And if I let you write what you like, the notebook . . . ?' She gestured to my bag.

I made a vanishing movement with my hand.

'The what? When contracts are signed, I'll hand it back, no copies made. I promise.'

'So you think it will be as easy as that? To write a book that destroys me?'

'It's just a story, Sofie.'

She nodded slowly, looking me up and down. Her blush had faded and she was once again porcelain-perfect.

'I never would have guessed you had it in you.'

'Well, you were the one that always told us fiction was just about getting away with something.'

The room became charged with a feeling that we were finally meeting as equals.

She took a step towards me, and I let her. When she put a hand on my shoulder, I didn't flinch. I could smell her perfume: pears and freesias. She leant in and pressed her lips against mine. Hers felt soft and powdery. I felt the power in that, in answering the question of what it would be like for her to be vulnerable, for once. I kissed her back, just for a moment, but her delicacy and tenderness were not what I really wanted. She was not who I wanted.

I stepped back and said, 'No.'

It seemed this was all she needed to hear. Perhaps she had learned something in the last few weeks.

'Well done, then, I suppose.' She looked at her watch. 'I have an interview. Someone for next year's cohort.'

I picked up my rucksack and slipped it over my shoulder as she turned back to her computer without saying goodbye.

I left her office and shut the door behind me. In the corridor there was a girl sitting on a chair, waiting to go in. She tilted her head towards me in expectation, and I smiled at her.

'Good luck,' I said.

'Do you have any tips?' she asked. She looked young for a master's student, her face plump like a fresh peach. I wanted to stroke the soft fur of her cheek and tell her to run. Her youth scared me, how ripe and available it was. I knew instantly that Sofie would love her.

'Just be yourself,' I said, hitching my rucksack further up my shoulder.

There was no way of explaining that now was the time to be yourself. Sooner or later, what made up who you were was replaced by the things you'd done. There was no essential you, only the choices you made when things happened, one after the other. It was best to be yourself for as long as possible, before you became a student, a woman scorned, or worst of all – a writer.

Bad Fiction

A debut author has found herself at the centre of an online literary debate after her novel was criticised in a series of reviews in the *Sunday Times*, the *Observer* and the *Telegraph*.

The novel, *Accused*, which was written on a Norwich-based creative writing course by author Alice Wootton, has been dismissed by prominent figures as 'a deeply unfeminist effort to capitalise on a literary witch-hunt.'

Reviews written by critics including Booker-prize shortlisted novelist Eleanor Crippon, express concern over 'pedestrian Creative Writing MA-speak' and a 'morally corrupt attempt to commodify the tabloid fodder' that surrounded prize-winning writer and mentor Sofie Muller. 'If the novel is dead,' Crippon wrote in her *Telegraph* review, 'then this book twisted the knife.'

The book's overwhelmingly negative critical reception has attracted widespread comment from the publishing industry on Twitter, including Muller herself, who remains in her post as Head of Creative Writing at the author's alma mater.

Accused charts the story of an undergraduate student accusing her professor of sexual assault, a plotline which bears more than the occasional similarity to the online accusations levelled at Muller herself two years ago, the same year Alice Wootton attended Muller's course. Various parties accused her of both sexual impropriety and plagiarism of students' work, but no official charges were ever brought due to lack of evidence.

Muller, who has repeatedly denied all accusations of both plagiarism and sexual misconduct, declared any veiled reference to her in *Accused* 'another example of the misogynistic literary teardown to which I have been subjected.'

While some online commenters have criticised the reviews as 'another example of the power established writers and academics continue to wield against newcomers, especially when they act as a group', others were quick to point out the 'hackneyed writing style' and 'crackpot feminism' of the novel in question.

While her ex-student's work comes under repeated attack, Muller's first novel in over a decade has stormed to the top of the *Sunday Times* bestseller list. *You Made Me Feel Like This* has been hailed as a 'revelatory take on class, consent and infidelity', telling the story of a factory worker who struggles to reconcile her roles as wife and mistress. Muller has hinted that the story was inspired by her early life before her literary success, which has led to critics applauding the book as a 'radical and brave approach to auto-fiction'. Muller herself said: 'My readers are used to my style of confessional writing. After twelve years, I'm back with my most revealing work yet.'

Alice Wootton has declined to comment.

Acknowledgments

I would like to thank my agent, Philippa Sitters, for all her instrumental help in the writing and publishing of this book. I would also like to thank the whole team at The Borough Press, notably Suzie Dooré, Jo Thompson and Jabin Ali, for their invaluable help in shaping this book into its final incarnation and getting it out into the world.

My own time studying creative writing was remarkably different from the events of this novel, and I would like to thank my tutors and friends who made my time at City University so rewarding. In particular to Van Mateo for constant encouragement and title inspiration for this book, and Sarah Tinsley, who read everything I ever wrote. I wish you could see this finished book – you are so missed.

I would also like to thank my family, who supported every stage of my writing this book. Particularly my mum, Les, Rick and Jacky for babysitting while I wrote and edited with a new baby.

Thanks to P, who came along with me at every point, and last but never, ever least, Theo, for everything.